"I shall only marry for love." Ariana smiled at him then and teased him a little. "Do you even know what that word means, Gian?"

"No," he replied, "and I don't care to find out."

For several reasons, that would not be a sensible thing to do. Neither was the way he was looking into her eyes right now.

Yes, he had noticed the huskiness of her voice and the earlier batting of her eyelashes. There was a friction in the Ariana-scented air, and his hand wanted to know for itself the softness of her cheek—so much so that Gian had to focus on not lifting his hand and cupping her face.

Gian, despite his formidable reputation, had scruples, and to kiss her, as he now desired to, was not something he would do.

And, aside from that, this was Ariana Romano.

The daughter of a man he respected and the little sister of his lifelong friend. An employee. A casual affair she could never be, and that was all Gian wanted or knew.

Ariana Romano was completely off-limits.

Carol Marinelli recently filled in a form asking for her job title. Thrilled to be able to put down her answer, she put "writer." Then it asked what Carol did for relaxation and she put down the truth— "writing." The third question asked for her hobbies. Well, not wanting to look obsessed, she crossed her fingers and answered "swimming"—but, given that the chlorine in the pool does terrible things to her highlights, I'm sure you can guess the real answer!

Books by Carol Marinelli

Harlequin Presents

Secret Prince's Christmas Seduction

One Night with Consequences

The Sicilian's Surprise Love-Child

Secret Heirs of Billionaires

Claimed for the Sheikh's Shock Son
Claiming His Hidden Heir

Ruthless Royal Sheikhs

Captive for the Sheikh's Pleasure

The Ruthless Deveraux Brothers

The Innocent's Shock Pregnancy
The Billionaire's Christmas Cinderella

Those Notorious Romanos

Italy's Most Scandalous Virgin

Visit the Author Profile page
at Harlequin.com for more titles.

Carol Marinelli

—

THE ITALIAN'S FORBIDDEN VIRGIN

PRESENTS

ISBN-13: 978-1-335-40355-1

The Italian's Forbidden Virgin

Copyright © 2021 by Carol Marinelli

Harlequin Enterprises ULC
22 Adelaide St. West, 40th Floor
Toronto, Ontario M5H 4E3, Canada
www.Harlequin.com

Printed in U.S.A.

THE ITALIAN'S
FORBIDDEN VIRGIN

CHAPTER ONE

GIAN DE LUCA WAS the Duke of Luctano, yet he chose not to use his title. Others, though, could not quite bring themselves to let it go.

And as he finished up the working week in his sumptuous office suite, on the ground floor of his flagship hotel La Fiordelise, in Rome, his PA informed him that his date—for want of a better word—had arrived.

'I was supposed to meet her at the theatre,' Gian said, barely looking up as he signed off on some paperwork.

'Yes,' Luna agreed, for she was more than aware of his heavy schedule and that he kept his private life and work as separate as was possible, 'and a driver was ordered, but it would seem she wanted...'

Luna paused for slight effect, which told Gian she was about to quote directly.

'"To save the Duke the trouble."'

His pen paused and then Gian's final signature

of the day appeared darkly on the page as the nib of his pen pressed in firmly. 'I see.'

'She also asked not to be treated as a hotel guest and made to wait in Reception. Given that pre-theatre dining is about to commence, she suggested meeting you in the restaurant.'

Gian held in a weary sigh. His restaurant was not a personal dining room for entertaining lovers. As soon as his dates started throwing around his title like confetti, or attempting to pull rank with his staff, or trying to get too familiar, it signalled the end for Gian. 'Tell her I'll be out shortly.'

'Except you have Ariana Romano in Reception waiting to see you.'

This time Gian could not hold in his sigh. His slate-grey eyes briefly shuttered as he braced himself for a mini-tornado, because it was always drama whenever she suddenly arrived.

If Ariana felt it, she said it.

'What does she want now?'

'A private matter, apparently.'

He kept his door open to her, given he was friends with her father Rafael and older brother Dante, in as much as Gian was friends with anyone. Growing up, he had been sent to Luctano each summer to stay with some distant aunt and her husband who, like his parents, hadn't much wanted him around. Those summers had often been spent hanging out with the Romanos.

Aside from the family ties, there were business connections too. Ariana was on the committee for the Romano Foundation Ball, which was held here at La Fiordelise each year. In small doses Gian chose to tolerate her, yet she was somewhat of an irritant. Rather like heavily scented jasmine in the flower arrangement in the foyer, or when lilies were left out just a little too long. Ariana had clung and irritated long after she had left and now, on a Friday evening, he had to deal with her in person.

'Bring her through then,' Gian said. 'Oh, and then take Svetlana through to the Pianoforte Bar to wait for me there...'

And there he would end their...*liaison*.

At thirty-five, Gian was considered one of Italy's most eligible bachelors.

His wealth and dark brooding looks were certainly a factor, but Gian was no fool and was aware that his title was coveted. He was the Duke of Luctano, even though his family had left the Tuscan hillsides generations ago and he had been born and raised in Rome. Or, rather, Gian had raised himself, for his hedonistic parents had had no time or inclination for their son.

Gian was, in fact, Italy's most *ineligible* bachelor for he had no interest in marriage or settling down and always stated up front with women that, apart from a handful of lavish dates, they would go no further than bed.

Gian had long ago decided that the De Luca lineage *would* end with him.

His sex life—Gian had never so much as contemplated the word 'love'—was rather like the stunning brass revolving doors at the entrance to La Fiordelise—wealth and beauty came in, was spoiled and pampered for the duration, but all too soon was ejected back out into the real world. Svetlana's behaviour was nothing unexpected: she had shown her true colours to his PA, and that was that.

They all did in the end.

Gian was jaded rather than bitter, and more than ready to get through this meeting with Ariana and then deal swiftly with Svetlana. So much so that he didn't bother to step into the luxury suite behind his office to freshen up for a night at Teatro dell'Opera; the gorgeous box with its pink-lined walls would remain empty tonight.

As would the luxurious suite behind his office.

His lovers never got so much as a toe in the door of his private apartment at La Fiordelise, for Gian was intensely private.

He sat drumming his fingers silently on his large black walnut desk, waiting for Ariana to arrive. But then, on a wintry and gloomy January evening, it was as if a vertical sunrise stepped into his office. Ariana's long black hair was slicked back into a low bun and she wore a suit and high heels. Except it was no ordinary suit. It was orange. The skirt sat just above the knee and the no doubt bespoke stockings were in exactly the same shade, as were the velvet stilettoes and large bag she carried over her shoulder. On most people the outfit would look ridiculous, but on pencil-thin Ariana it looked tasteful and bright…like a streak of burnt gold on the horizon heralding a new day.

Gian refused to be dazzled and reminded himself of the absolute diva she was. Ariana was the one who should be performing at Teatro dell'Opera tonight!

'Gian,' she purred, and gave him her signature red-lipped smile. It was the same smile that set the cameras flashing on the red carpets in Rome, but Gian remained steadfastly unimpressed—not that he showed it, for he was more than used to dealing with the most pampered guests.

'Ariana.' He pushed back his chair to stand and greet her. 'You look amazing as always.' He said all the right things, though could not help but add, 'Very orange.'

'Cinnamon, Gian,' she wryly corrected as her heart did the oddest thing.

It stopped.

Gian *should* be familiar. After all, she had known him all her life, yet she was suddenly reminded of his height and the deep tone of his voice. He wore a subtly checked suit in grey with a waistcoat, though his height meant that he wore the check rather than the check wearing him.

Of course her heart had started again—had it not she would have dropped to the floor—but it was jumping around in some ungainly trot as he walked towards her.

Pure nerves, Ariana decided. After all, she did have a huge favour to ask!

'I apologise for not coming out to greet you,' Gian said as he came around the desk and kissed her on both cheeks. 'I was just finishing up some work.'

'That's fine. Luna took good care of me.'

Except she felt far from fine. Ariana rather wished that the nerves in her chest would abate, yet they fluttered like butterflies—or perhaps fireflies would be a more apt description because there was a flash of heat creeping up her neck and searing her cheeks, but then Gian was, to say the least, rather commanding.

Cold, people called him.

Especially back home in Luctano, where gossip and rumour abounded. The history of the De Lucas was often whispered about and discussed in her home town—at times even by her family. Though a child at the time, Ariana could well remember the shock and horror in the village as news of the fire aboard their luxury yacht had hit in the early hours of a Sunday morning. And, of course, she still remembered the funeral held in Luctano for the Duke, the Duchess and the heir apparent…

People whispered about the fact that Luca hadn't attended the renewal of his parents' vows, and his lack of visible emotion at the funeral.

Yet, as Ariana sometimes pointed out, the fact that he hadn't attended had saved his life.

And, the villagers would add, happy to twist the truth, *his brother's death made him a duke.* As if Gian had swum out into the ocean and torched the boat himself!

'Basta!' Ariana would tell them.

Enough!

Ariana actually *liked* his steely reserve.

Her own self was so volatile that when life spun too fast, it was to Gian she turned for his distant, measured ways.

While rumour had it he melted women in the bedroom and endeared both staff and guests with his calm assertiveness, it was the general consensus that behind his polished façade there was no heart or emotion, just a wall of solid black ice. Ariana needed that wall of black ice on side so she kept her smile bright. 'Thank you for agreeing to see me.'

'Of course.' Gian gestured for her to take a seat as he did the same. 'Can I offer you some refreshments?'

'No, thank you.' Gosh, small talk was difficult when you had a huge favour to ask! 'How was your Christmas?'

'Busy,' Gian responded, then politely enquired, 'Yours?'

Ariana lifted her hand and made a wavering gesture, to show it had not been the best, though she did not bore Gian with the details, like how, in the manner of a tennis ball in an extended rally, she'd bounced between Florence and Rome. Gian already knew all about her parents' divorce and her father's subsequent marriage to the much younger Mia. After all the marriage had taken place here!

And he knew too that her father wasn't at home in Luctano but in a private hospital in Florence and so she gave him a brief update. 'Dante is hoping to have Papà moved here to Rome,' Ariana said, but left out the *hospice* word. 'That should make things a bit easier.'

'Easier for whom?' Gian enquired.

'For his family,' Ariana responded tartly, but then squirmed inwardly, for it was the very question she had been asking herself since her brothers had suggested the move. 'His children are all here, his Rome office...' Her voice trailed off. Though the impressive Romano Holdings offices were in the EUR business district of Rome, Dante had taken over the running of the company when their father had remarried.

Gian's question was a pertinent one—and confirmed for Ariana that she needed to speak with her father and find out exactly what it was *he* wanted for the final months of his life. 'It is not all decided,' she admitted to Gian. 'We are just testing ideas.'

'Good,' Gian said, and she blinked at the gentler edge to his tone. 'I visited him yesterday.'

'You visited him in Florence?'

'Of course. You know I have a sister hotel opening there in May?' Gian checked, and Ariana nodded. 'I always try and drop in on Rafael when I am there.'

For some reason that brought the threat of tears to her eyes, but she hastily blinked them back. Ariana was not one for tears—well, not real ones; crocodile tears she excelled at—but at times Florence, where her father was in hospital, felt so far away. It was an hour or so by plane and she visited as much as she could. So did her brothers, and of course Mia was there and the family home in Luctano was nearby...

but at night, when she couldn't sleep, Ariana always thought of her father alone.

There was a break in the conversation that Gian did absolutely nothing to fill. A pregnant pause was something Ariana was incapable of. If there was a gap she felt duty-bound to speak. Any lull in proceedings and she felt it her place to perform. Gian, she felt, would let this silence stretch for ever and so of course it was she who ended it. 'Gian, there is a reason I am here…'

Of course there was!

Her slender hands twisted in her lap. She was nervous, Gian realised. This was most unlike Ariana, who was usually supremely confident—arrogant, in fact. It dawned on him then what this urgent appointment might be about. Did she want to bring her latest lover here, without it being billed to the Romano guest folio so as to avoid her father or brothers finding out?

It was often the case with family accounts, but if that was what Ariana was about to ask him…

No way!

There was no question he would facilitate her bringing her latest lover to stay here! 'What is it you want?' Gian asked, and she blinked at the edge to his tone.

'I have decided that I want a career.'

'A career?' His features relaxed and there was

even a shadow of a smile that he did not put down to relief that she wasn't intending to bring her lover here. It was typical of Ariana to say she wanted a career, rather than a job. 'Really?'

'Yes.' She nodded. 'I've given it a great deal of thought.'

'And your career of choice?'

'I would like to be Guest Services Manager here at La Fiordelise. Or rather I would like to be Guest Services Manager for your VIPs.'

'All of my guests are VIPs, Ariana.'

'You *know* what I mean.'

He had to consciously resist rolling his eyes. 'Why would I simply hand you such a position when you have no experience? Why would I let you near my VIPs?'

'Because I am one!' Ariana retorted, but then rather hurriedly checked herself. 'What I am trying to say is that I know their ways. Please, Gian. I really want this.'

Gian knew very well that whatever Ariana wanted, Ariana got—until she grew bored and dismissed it. Ariana should have been put over her father's knee many years ago and learned the meaning of the word 'no'. There was no way on God's earth that she was going to *play* careers at his hotel. So, rather than go through the motions, he shook his head. 'Ariana, let me stop you right there. While I appreciate—'

'Actually,' she cut in swiftly, 'I *would* like some refreshments after all. Perhaps, given the hour, some champagne is in order.' Her pussy-cat smile was triumphant as she prevented him ending their conversation.

Ever the consummate host, Gian nodded politely. *'Naturalmente.'* He pressed the intercom. 'Luna, would you please bring in champagne for myself and Ariana.'

Ariana's smile remained. No doubt, Gian assumed, she was thinking she had won, but what she did not quite understand was that Gian was always and absolutely one step ahead. Luna had worked at La Fiordelise even before his family had died and knew his nuances well. It was often what was *not* said that counted, and right at this moment Vincenzo, the bar manager, would be pouring two *glasses* of French champagne.

A bottle and ice bucket would *not* be arriving.

This was no tête-à-tête.

'I have brought my résumé,' Ariana said, digging in her suede designer *cinnamon* bag and producing a document, which she handed to him. He took it without a word and as he read through it, Gian found again that he fought an incredulous smile.

For someone who had practically never worked a day in her life, Ariana Romano had an impressive résumé indeed.

At least, it *read* well. She had studied hospital-ity and tourism management, although he knew that already. Naturally, she was on the Romano Board, and on the Romano Foundation Board too.

As well as that were listed all the luncheons, balls and functions which Ariana claimed to have planned and organised singlehandedly. Except—

'Ariana, you do not "create, design and imple-ment the theme for the annual Romano Foun-dation Ball",' Gian said, and used his fingers to quote directly from her résumé. 'My staff do.'

'Well, I have major input.'

'No, Ariana, you don't. In fact, you barely show up for the meetings.'

'I always attend.'

'I can have Luna retrieve the minutes of them if you like. You rarely show up and you don't even bother to send an apology. The fact is you consistently let people down.'

'Excuse me!' Ariana reared, unused to him speaking so harshly, for, though cold, Gian was always polite.

Except here, today, they had entered unknown territory.

Usually when they discussed the Romano Ball, given the fact she was Rafael's daughter, Ariana's suggestions were tolerated, lauded even. Now, though, Gian refused to play the usual game of applauding her inaction, or nodding as she reeled off one of her less-than-well-thought-out ideas. He picked last year's ball as an example. 'You said you were thinking "along the lines of silver" and no doubt went off to plan your gown.'

He watched her lips press tightly together. Even clamped shut, Ariana had a very pretty mouth, but he quickly dragged his attention away from that thought and back to the point he was trying to make. 'Following your suggestion, my staff created a silver world, whereas you did nothing more than turn up on the night...' he held her angry gaze '...in a silver gown.'

'How nice that you remember what I was wearing,' Ariana retorted.

'Call it an educated guess.'

Ouch!

Suddenly, under his withering gaze, in this private meeting she had demanded, Ariana felt as gauche and naive as the virgin she was, rather than the temptress she portrayed. 'Well, I was the one who came up with a forest theme for this year,' Ariana reminded him.

'Tell me,' Gian pushed, 'what have you done to help implement the forest theme, apart from choose the fabric for your gown?'

Ariana opened her mouth to answer and then closed it. He watched her shoulders briefly slump in defeat, but then she rallied. 'I suggested ivy around the pillars in the ballroom.'

He looked as unimpressed with her suggestion as he had at the board meeting, Ariana thought. But, then, Gian considered decorations and themes and such somewhat vulgar.

'And berries,' Ariana hurriedly. 'I suggested a berry dessert. Fruits of the forest...'

Gian did not so much as blink; he just stared at her pretty, empty head.

Only...that wasn't right, and he knew it.

Ariana, when she so chose, was perceptive and clever, but he refused to relent. 'What about last month, December, the hotel's busiest time, and you reserved the Pianoforte Bar for yourself and your friends' exclusive use, yet forgot to let Reservations know that it was no longer required.'

'You were paid,' Ariana interrupted. 'My father—'

'Precisely.' It was Gian who now interrupted. '*Your father* took care of things. It is so very typical of you, Ariana. If something better comes along, then that is where your attention goes.'

'No!' Ariana shook her head, angrily at first but then in sudden bewilderment because he was usually so polite. 'Why are you speaking to me like this, Gian?'

'So that you understand completely why my answer to your request is no.'

It sounded as if he meant it, and Ariana wasn't particularly used to that so she tried another tack. 'I studied hospitality and—'

'I know you did.' Again, Gian cut her off. 'You might remember that it was necessary for you to do three months' work experience to pass your course and so I spoke to your father and offered for you to do your placement here.' His eyes never left her face. 'You failed to show up on your starting day.'

Ariana flushed. 'Because I decided to do my placement at the family hotel in Luctano.'

'And you didn't even think to let me know?'

'I thought my father's staff had contacted you.'

But Gian shook his head. 'The fact is, Ariana, you chose the easier option.'

'I wanted to work here, Gian,' Ariana insisted. 'But my parents wanted me at the family hotel.'

'No.' Gian shook his head, refusing to accept her twisted truth. 'You declined when I explained that your placement would consist of *working* in all areas of the hotel. You were to spend a week in the kitchen, a week as a chambermaid, a week—'

It was Ariana who interrupted now, her voice fighting not to rise as she cut in. 'I felt I would get more experience in Luctano.'

'Really?' Gian checked. 'You thought you would get more experience at a small boutique resort in the Tuscan hills than at an award-winning, five-star hotel in the heart of Rome?'

'Yes,' she attempted. 'Well, perhaps not as extensive as I would have had here but…' Her voice trailed off because her excuse was as pathetic as it sounded, but there was another reason entirely that his offer to work at La Fiordelise had been declined all those years ago. 'That wasn't the only reason I said no, Gian. The fact is, my mother didn't want me working here.'

'Why ever not?'

Even as she opened her mouth to speak, even as the words tumbled out, Ariana knew she should never be saying them. 'Because of your reputation with women.'

CHAPTER TWO

'Pardon?'

Gian was supremely polite as he asked her to repeat her accusation, but far from backtracking or apologising, Ariana clarified her words.

'My mother didn't want me working here because of your reputation with women.' She didn't even blush as she said it. If anything, she was defiant.

Still, such was the sudden tension that it was a relief when there was a knock on the door and soon Luna was placing down little white coasters decorated with La Fiordelise's swirling rose gold insignia and two long, pale flutes of champagne, as well as a little silver dish of nibbles.

The dish in itself was beautiful, heavy silver with three little heart-shaped trays, individually filled with nuts, slivers of fruit and chocolates.

It was easier to focus on incidentals because, despite her cool demeanour, Ariana could feel the crackle in the air that denoted thunder, and as the door closed on Luna, she stared at the pretty dish as she re-crossed her legs at the ankles.

'Ariana.' Gian's voice was seemingly smooth but there was a barbed edge to his tone that tempted her to retrieve her bag and simply run. Gian carried on, 'Before we continue this conversation, can I make one thing supremely clear?'

'Of course,' Ariana said. Unable to look at him any longer, she reached for a glass.

'Your mother had no right to imply or suggest that I would be anything other than professional with the work experience girl—or, in fact, any of my staff!'

'Well, you do have a formidable reputation…' Ariana started and raised the glass to her lips.

'With *women*,' Gian interrupted and then tartly added, 'Not teenage girls, which you were back *then*.'

Ariana nodded, the glass still hovering by her mouth. Even as he told her off, even as he scolded her for going too far, there was something else that had been said there—that she was different now compared to then.

She was a woman.

And Gian De Luca was a very good-looking man.

She had known that, of course. His undoubtedly handsome looks had always been there—something she had registered, but only at a surface level. Yet today it had felt as if she'd been handed a pair of magical eyeglasses and she wanted to weep as she saw colour for the first time.

He was beautiful.

Exquisitely so.

His jet-black hair framed a haughty face, and his mouth, though unsmiling, was plump in contrast to the razor-sharp cheekbones and straight nose.

She could not be in lust with Gian *and* work for him—that would never ever do!

She wanted to pull off those imaginary glasses, to be plunged back into a monotone world, where Gian De Luca was just, well…

Gian.

Not a name she wanted to roll on her tongue.

Not a mouth she now wanted to taste.

He was just Gian, she reminded herself.

The person she ran to when trouble loomed large.

She put her glass down on the small coaster as she attempted to push her inappropriate thoughts aside and rescue the interview. 'Mamma didn't mean it, Gian. You know what she can be like…'

'Yes.' Gian held in a pained sigh. 'I do.'

Too well he recalled joining the Romanos at their dinner table as a small boy. *'Straccione,'*

Angela would say, ruffling his hair as he took a seat at the table. It had sounded like an affectionate tease; after all, how could the son of a duke and duchess be a ragamuffin and a beggar?

Except Angela had found the cruellest knife to dig into his heart, and she knew how to twist it, for Gian had always felt like a beggar for company.

Gian wasn't quite sure why Angela rattled him so much.

Ariana did too, albeit it in an increasingly different way.

He did not want Ariana working here. And not just because of her precious ways but because of this…this pull, this awareness, this attraction that did not sit well with him. 'Let's just leave things there, shall we?' he suggested. 'While we're still able to be civil. I could put you in touch with the director at Hotel Rav—' He went to name his closest rival but Ariana cut in even before he had finished.

'I was already offered a job there, and in several other hotels as well, but each time it was in return for some media coverage. I really don't want cameras following me on my first day.'

'Fair enough.' While he understood that, the rest he didn't get. 'What *are* you hoping to achieve by this, Ariana?'

'More than I am right now,' she said, and gave a hollow laugh.

He looked at her then.

Properly looked.

Ariana was, of course, exquisitely beautiful, with a delicate bone structure, but he suddenly noticed that rather than the trademark black eyes of her father and brothers, or the icy blue ones of her mother, Ariana's eyes were a deep navy-violet, almost as if they'd tried to get from blue to black, but had surrendered just shy of arrival.

Gian rather wished he hadn't noticed the beguiling colour of them and rapidly diverted his gaze back to her résumé.

'Why don't you formally interview me?' Ariana suggested. 'As if we don't know each other. Surely you can do that?'

'Of course, but if you want an honest interview, what happens if you are not successful?' She wouldn't be, he knew, but as he looked up she held his gaze as she answered.

'Then I shall walk away, knowing I tried.'

Walk away, Gian wanted to warn her, for there was a sudden energy between them that could never end well.

He scanned through her supposed work experience and attempted to wipe out a lifetime of history so they could face each other as two strangers. In the end, he reverted to his usual interview technique. 'Tell me about a recent time when you had to deal with a difficult client or contact...'

She wouldn't be able to, Gian was certain.

'Well...' Ariana thought for a moment. 'I wanted an interview with the owner of a very prestigious hotel, but I did not want to utilise my family contacts as I felt that would do me no favours.'

Gian felt his lips tighten when it became clear that she was speaking about trying to get in contact with him. 'Ariana,' he cut in, 'may I suggest that you don't make the person interviewing you the *difficult contact*.'

'But he was difficult. My goal was to get a full audience,' Ariana continued, 'and so I sent in my résumé, but when I heard nothing back...'

'You sent in an application?' Gian started scrolling through his computer, *almost* apologetic now, because an application from Ariana Romano *should* have been flagged—at the very least so he could personally reject her. 'Vanda has been on leave over the festive period...' He paused, for he could find nothing. 'When did you send it?'

'This morning,' Ariana replied, and then took a sip of her champagne.

'This morning.' Gian sighed, and leaned back in his chair. He looked upon the epitome of instant gratification. When Ariana wanted something she wanted it now!

'So, when I heard nothing back, I printed off my résumé and took it to him personally.'

'And what was the result?'

'I made him smile,' Ariana said.

'No,' Gian corrected, 'you didn't.'

'Almost.'

'Not even close.' He let out a breath as he tried to hold onto patience. 'Ariana, you asked for a proper interview, so treat it as if we've never met. Now, tell me about a time you were able to deal successfully with another person even when you may not have liked them.'

'Okay…' She chewed her bottom lip and thought for less than a moment. 'My father was recently given a terminal diagnosis. He still has months to live,' she added rather urgently, 'but…' She swallowed, for Ariana could not bear to think of a time months from now and dragged her mind back to the present. 'I am not a fan of his new wife.'

'Ariana, I am asking about professional—'

'However,' she cut in, 'I spoke calmly to her and said that I would like to be part of all interviews with the doctors and that for his sake, we should at least be polite.'

Curiosity got the better of him. 'How is that working out?'

She gave a snooty sniff and re-crossed her legs. 'We've both kept our sides of the agreement.'

Gian rather doubted it. Ariana and Mia were a toxic mix indeed! 'I was actually hoping you could give me examples that involve work, Ariana.'

'Oh, believe me,' she countered. 'Mia is work.'

Gian just wanted this charade over and done with. Both their glasses were nearly empty so he would ask one more question and then send her on her precocious way. 'Tell me about a time where you did something for someone else, not to earn favour, and without letting them know.'

'That would defeat the purpose,' Ariana deftly answered, 'if I later use it in an interview to show how benevolent I am.'

He liked her answer. In fact, were it a real interview, it might score her points, except he wasn't sure that Ariana wasn't simply being evasive. 'It's an important question, Ariana,' he told her. 'The role of Guest Services is to make a stay at La Fiordelise appear seamlessly unique. The aim is that our guests never know the work that goes on behind the scenes. So,' he added, 'I would like an honest answer.'

'Very well.' She was hesitant, though, for to tell him revealed more than she cared to. 'My brother...' She tried to remember that this was an interview and she should treat Gian as if he were a stranger. 'My twin brother, Stefano, is to marry soon—at the end of May.'

'And?'

'I have been somewhat excluded from the wedding plans.'

'Despite your extensive planning experience,' he added rather drily.

'Despite that!' Ariana answered crisply. 'They have decided that they don't need my help.'

He saw the jut of her chin and that her hands were rigid in her lap, and suddenly Gian did not like the question he had asked, for he could see it was hurting her to answer.

'Eloa,' Ariana continued, 'Stefano's fiancée, had her heart set on the wedding being held at Palazzo Pamphili…'

'Where the Brazilian Embassy is housed.' Gian nodded. He knew it well, for the superb building was across the square from the hotel, and even with his connections he knew how hard it would be to arrange a wedding there.

'I sorted it,' Ariana said.

'How?' Gian frowned, quietly impressed.

'That is for me to know,' Ariana responded. 'However, to this day, Eloa and Stefano think that they arranged the reception venue by themselves.'

'You haven't told them that you were behind it?'

'No. They have made it clear they don't want my help and it might sour things for them to know I had a hand in it.'

She watched as he put down her résumé and she continued to watch his long fingers join and arch into a steeple. He slowly drew a breath and Ariana felt certain that he had not been persuaded, and that she was about to be told that his answer was still no. 'I really do want to work, Gian.' There was a slightly frantic note to her voice, which she fought to quash, but there was also desperation in her eyes that she could not hide. 'I love the hotel industry and, you're right, I should have done my placement here…' It wasn't just that, though. 'I want some real independence. I'm tired of—' She stopped herself, sure that Gian did not need to hear it.

Yet he found that he wanted to. 'Go on,' Gian invited, casting his more regular interview technique aside.

'I'm tired of living in an apartment my family owns, tired of being on call when my mother decides I can drop everything for her. After all,' she mimicked a derisive tone, 'I couldn't *possibly* be busy.' She screwed her eyes closed in frustration, unable to properly explain the claustrophobic feeling of her privileged world.

Oh, many might say that life had been handed to Ariana Romano on a plate.

The trouble was, it wasn't necessarily a feast of her choosing.

While she had a family who seemingly adored her, even as a child Ariana had always been told to take her toys and play somewhere else.

To this day it persisted.

While she had access to wealth most people could only dream of, there was a perpetual feeling of emptiness. For Ariana, the golden cup she drank from was so shot through with holes that no gifts—no trust-funded central Rome apartment, no wild party, no designer outfit or A-list appearance—filled her soul.

'I want a career,' Ariana insisted.

'Why now?' Gian pushed.

'It's a new year, a time when everyone takes stock…' She suddenly looked beyond Gian to the window behind him and saw white flakes dance in the darkness. 'It is starting to snow.'

'Don't change the subject,' Gian said, without so much as turning his head to take in the weather. It was Ariana he was more interested in. 'Why now, Ariana?'

Because I'm lonely, she wanted to say.

Because before Mia came along, I thought I had something of a career at Romano Holdings.

Because my days are increasingly empty and there surely has to be more to life than this?

Of course, she could not answer with that, and so she took a breath and attempted a more dignified response. 'I want to make something of myself, by myself. I want, for a few hours a day, to take off the Romano name. Look, I know what I'm asking is a favour, but—'

'Let me stop you right there,' he cut in. 'I don't do favours.'

There was from Ariana a slight, almost inaudible laugh, yet Gian understood its wry gist and conceded. 'Perhaps I make concessions for your father, but he was very good to me when...'

Gian didn't finish but Ariana knew he was referring to when his brother and parents had died and, to her nosy shame, Ariana hoped to hear more. 'When what?' she asked, as if she didn't know.

Nobody did silence better than Gian.

Surely, not a soul on this earth was as comfortable with silence as he, for he just stared right back at her and refused to elaborate.

It was Ariana who filled the long gap. 'I didn't get my father to lean on you, Gian,' she pointed out. 'I'm trying my best to do this by myself.'

'I know that,' Gian admitted, for if she had asked her father to call in a favour, then Rafael would have had a quiet word with him when he'd visited yesterday.

'I won't let you down, Gian.'

But even with Ariana's assurances, Gian was hesitant. He did not want Ariana to be his problem. He did not need the complication of hiring and, no doubt, having to fire her. And yet, *and yet*, he grudgingly admired her attempt to make something of herself, aside from the family name she'd been born into.

She broke into his thoughts then. 'Perhaps you could show me around?'

'I do not give guided tours to potential staff, that is Vanda's domain…'

'Ah, so I'm "potential staff" now?'

'I did not say that.'

'Then, as a family friend, you can show me around.'

Gian took a breath, and looked into navy violet eyes and better understood the predicament her parents must find themselves in at times. How the hell did you say no to that?

CHAPTER THREE

To THE SURPRISE of both of them, Gian agreed to
the tour of La Fiordelise.

Ariana's clear interest in the hotel pleased him,
and if it had been a real interview, her request
would have impressed him indeed.

'Just a short tour...' he nodded '...given you
are my final appointment for the day.'

Perhaps it was the single glass of champagne
on a nervously empty stomach, but Ariana was
giddy with excitement as she stood up. There was
even a heady thought that perhaps they might
conclude the tour in the restaurant, and then dinner, of course.

And there Gian would offer her the role of VIP
Guest Services Manager!

Oh, she could just picture herself in the bespoke blush tartan suits and pearls that the guest
services managers wore!

It felt very different walking through the foyer
with Gian at her side. Ariana was more than used

to turning heads, but there was a certain deference that Gian commanded. Staff straightened at his approach, and guests nudged each other when he passed. There was a certain *something* about Gian that was impossible to define. Something more than elegance, more than command.

Ariana would like to name it.

To bottle it.

To dab her wrists with the essence he emanated.

Soon they had passed Reception and the Pianoforte Bar where, unbeknownst to Ariana, Svetlana sat drumming her fingers on the table, her silver platter of nuts empty, as was her glass. Vincenzo was taking care of that, though, and shaking another cocktail for her, yet Gian barely gave her a glance. He was working after all.

'You know the Pianoforte Bar…' Gian said rather drily, thinking of the array of colour Ariana and her friends made as they breezed in on a Friday night for cocktails to get the weekend underway. 'No doubt your friend Nicki shall be here soon.'

'She shan't be,' Ariana said. 'Nicki is away, skiing with friends.'

'Don't you usually go?'

'Yes, but I didn't want to be stuck on a mountain with Papà so unwell so I told them to go ahead without me.'

'They're staying at the Romano chalet?'

'Of course.' Ariana gave a tight shrug. 'Just because I can't go it doesn't mean I should let everyone down. It's our annual trip.'

That took place on her dime, Gian thought.

He loathed her hangers-on, and all too often had to hold his tongue when her entitled, self-important friends arrived at La Fiordelise courtesy of her name.

He could not hold his tongue now. 'Your partner was asked to leave here the other week.'

'My partner?' Ariana frowned, wondering who he meant. 'Oh, you mean Paulo…'

'I don't know his name,' Gian lied.

Absolutely he knew his name, and those of her so-called friends who added their drinks to the Romano tab, even when Ariana was not here. Gian had even spoken to Rafael about it and had been disappointed with his response: 'Any friend of Ariana's…'

Could Rafael not see his daughter was being used? No, because in his declining years it was easier for Rafael not to see!

'Paulo was never my partner,' Ariana cut in. 'He and I, well…' She shrugged, uncertain how to describe them. 'It's just business, I guess.'

'Business?' Gian checked.

'The business of being seen.'

Oh, Ariana…

Still, she was not here for life advice, so Gian brushed his fleeting sympathy aside and got on with the tour.

'This is the Terazza Suite. It caters for up to thirty and is used for smaller, very exclusive functions…'

'Is this where my father married *her*?' Ariana asked, refusing to use Mia's name. She had been invited to the wedding, but of course neither she nor her brothers had chosen to attend.

'Yes,' Gian said, without elaborating about the wedding. 'It opens out to a terrace adjacent to the square, though it is too cold to go out there now.'

'I would like to see it.'

The Terazza Suite was empty, but it took little imagination to see that the gold stencilled walls and high ceilings would make a romantic venue indeed.

One wall was lined with French windows and when she pushed down on a handle Ariana found that of course it was locked. *'Per favore?'* she asked. She sensed his reluctance, but Gian first pressed a discreet alarm on the wall then took out his master key and unlocked a door.

As she stepped out it was not the frigid air that caught her breath, more the beauty of the surroundings. There was the chatter and laughter from the square, which was visible through an ornate fence.

'In spring and summer there is a curtain of wisteria that blocks the noise,' Gian explained, looking up at the naked vines, 'but it can be dressed for privacy in winter.' He told her about a recent Christmas wedding with boxed firs for privacy, only Ariana wasn't really listening.

Instead, her silence was borne of regret for not being here to support her father...

'Certainly,' Gian continued, 'it is perfect for more intimate gatherings...'

'You mean weddings that no one wants to attend,' Ariana said, shame and regret making her suddenly defensive.

'You are showing your age, Ariana,' Gian said.

'My age?' Ariana frowned as they stepped back into the warmth and he locked up behind them. 'I'm twenty-five.'

'I meant in brat years,' Gian said, and left her standing there, mouth gaping in indignation as he marched on, just wanting this tour to be over. 'You already know the ballroom...' He waved in its general direction as she caught up, but Ariana had more than a ballroom on her mind.

'Did you just call me a brat?' She couldn't quite believe what he had said.

'Yes,' he said. 'I did.'

'You can't talk to me like that.'

'You're almost right. Once I employ you I can't

tell you what an insufferable, spoilt little madam you are…'

But though most people would have burst into tears at his tone, Gian knew Ariana better than that. Instead he watched her red lips part into a smile as realisation hit. 'You're going to take me on, then?'

'I haven't quite decided yet,' Gian said. 'Come on.'

'But I want to see the ballroom.'

'They are in the final preparations for a function tonight.'

'I would so love to see how others do it,' she said, ignoring Gian and opening one of the heavy, ornate doors and gasping when she peeked in. 'Oh, it looks so beautiful.'

'It is a fortieth wedding anniversary celebration,' Gian told her.

'Ruby,' Ariana sighed, for the tables were dressed with deep red roses and they were in the middle of a final test of the lighting so that even the heavy chandeliers cast rubies of light around the room with stunning effect. 'I know I get angry about my parents' divorce,' she admitted—although as she gazed into the ballroom it was almost as if she was speaking to herself— 'and it is not all Mia's fault, I accept that, but I was always so proud of their marriage. Of course, it was not *my* achievement, but I was so proud of them for still being together when so many marriages fail...'

She gave him pause. Gian looked at her as she spoke, and could almost see the stars in her eyes as she gazed at the gorgeous ballroom.

'I should have gone to Papà's wedding,' Ariana said, for the first time voicing her private remorse. 'I deeply regret that I stayed away.'

Gian was rarely torn to break a confidence. The truth was, Rafael had been relieved that his children had not attended the nuptials. It was a marriage in name only, a brief service, followed by drinks on the terrace, then a cake and kiss for the cameras...

As the owner of several prestigious hotels, Gian was the keeper of many secrets.

So outrageous were the many scandals that Gian was privy to that the Romanos and their rather reprobate ways barely registered a blip. But it would be a seismic event if Ariana found out the truth about her parents.

Their marriage had been over long before their divorce.

Angela Romano had been with her lover for decades. Prior to the divorce, Angela and Thomas had often enjoyed extended midweek breaks at La Fiordelise.

Rafael would not blink an eye if he knew; in fact, Gian, assumed that he did. For those long business lunches Rafael had enjoyed with Roberto—his lawyer—had, in fact, been rare public outings for a devoted couple who had been together for more than fifteen years.

As for Mia...

Well, Gian to this day did not understand Angela's hatred towards her, when close friends all knew that Mia was Rafael's beard—a prop used to prevent the world from finding out in his declining years that Rafael Romano was gay. Perhaps, if Ariana could have this necessary conversation with her father, it might lead him to reveal his truth before it was too late or, worse, before she inadvertently found out.

'Why don't you tell your father that you regret not being at his wedding?' Gian suggested. 'Talk to him about it...'

'I try to stay upbeat when I visit him.'

'Tell him how you feel,' Gian gently pushed, and saw that she was thinking about it.

'I might.' She nodded and then turned to him with a question no one had ever dared ask. 'Were your parents happy?'

It was just a question, and it flowed from the context perhaps, but he had to think for a long moment, to cast his mind back, to the parties, to the laughter, to the inappropriate mess that had been them, and for once he did not choose silence. 'Yes,' Gian finally answered. 'They were happy because they followed only their hearts and not their heads.' When she frowned, clearly nonplussed, Gian explained further. 'Their happiness was to the exclusion of all else.'

'Including you?'

He did not answer and Ariana knew she had crossed the line, but now they were in this odd standoff.

They looked at each other. His thick black hair was so superbly cut that as she looked up at him she felt the oddest temptation to raise her hand and simply touch it, and to see if it fell back into perfect shape, but of course impulse had no place here, and anyway it was just a thought. But that made it a red button that said *do not touch*, and consequently made her itch to do so. 'Including you?' she persisted.

'This is an interview, Ariana, the purpose of which is to find out more about you, not the other way around.'

Under her breath she muttered, 'Your life is an interview then.'

'Pardon?'

'It just dawned on me, Gian, that you know an awful lot about me, but I know practically nothing about you.'

'Good,' he clipped.

It wasn't good, though. Suddenly there was a whole lot that Ariana wanted to know about him, and her heart suddenly stopped with its ungainly trot and kicked into a gallop.

He angered her.

Only that wasn't quite right, because anger didn't make her thighs suddenly clamp, or her lips ache. And anger didn't make her knickers damp or give her an urge to kiss that haughty, arrogant face. This was something else entirely, though her voice when she spoke was indeed cross. 'Are you going to hire me or not, Gian?'

'I am hesitant to.'

While he wanted to afford her a new start, Ariana working here spelt Trouble.

In more ways than one.

Yes, she was airy and spoilt and brattish, but he could almost feel the prickle of her under his skin and that was an attraction that was safer to deny. 'If it doesn't work out—' he started.

'It *will* work out,' she broke in. 'I shall make it so!'

And I will push all thoughts of fancying you aside, Ariana hurriedly thought.

'You would still have to do the twelve-week induction.' He wasn't asking, he was telling. 'It is mandatory that all my guest services staff have personally worked in every area of the hotel.'

'Yes.' Ariana nodded. 'I'll do the induction.'

'If you are successful in your introductory period then there might be a position as a guest services *assistant*...'

'But—'

'My managers earn their titles, Ariana.' He watched two spots of colour start to burn on her cheeks. 'And there will be no favours and no concessions. From this point on, the trajectory of your career is in your hands. You will report on Monday at seven to Vanda, who deals with staff training, and any issues you have, you take to her, not me.'

'Of course.'

He wasn't sure she got it, though. 'Ariana, this is my hotel, and I separate things, so if you work here you must understand that I don't deal with the grumbles of minor staff. I don't want to hear about your day; I simply do not want to know. I don't want to hear you can't handle vomit or difficult guests. You take it up with Vanda. Not my problem...'

'Of course.'

'And there shall be no stopping by my office for champagne. That stops today! In fact, as of now there will be no need to drop by my office at all.'

She pouted. 'You said I could always come to you.'

He had.

And over the years *she* had.

Not all her confessionals took place in his office, though. They went way further back than that.

Once in Luctano, an eight-year-old Ariana, too scared to confide in her older brother Dante, had admitted to an eighteen-year-old Gian that she had stolen chocolate from the local store. She wouldn't tell him why, just pleaded with him not to tell her father or Dante.

'First, explain to me why you stole,' Gian had persisted. 'You have the money to pay.'

'Stefano dared me to,' Ariana had admitted. 'I haven't eaten it, though. The chocolate is still under my bed, but I feel ill when I try to say my prayers…'

Gian had taken her in to the store and Ariana had duly apologised and paid for the chocolate, and, no, he had not told Dante or Rafael. Instead he'd had a quiet word with Stefano. 'You want to steal,' he had said to the young boy, 'then at least have the guts to do it yourself.'

Another time, some years later, Stefano had been caught smoking and Ariana had arrived here in Gian's office and begged him to impersonate her father when the school inevitably rang.

'Why would they ring here?' Gian had frowned.

'Because I told Stefano to say that Papà is here at La Fiordelise on business.'

Ariana was a minx and far too skilled at lying. Gian had of course declined to cover for Stefano, and had spoken to Rafael himself.

There was *always* drama surrounding Ariana, though it was not always of her own making— just two years ago, in the midst of her parents' scandalous divorce, she had found out that her father was ill and Ariana had sat in Gian's office, being fed tissues but not false promises.

Yes, he had kept his door open to her, but—

'If I hire you,' Gian said, very carefully, 'all that stops.'

And suddenly, if the safety net of Gian was going to be removed, Ariana didn't know if she wanted her career any more—not that he seemed to notice her dilemma.

'Who the hell orders champagne at a job interview?' Gian mused.

'It was my first ever interview,' Ariana admitted. 'I sensed your irritation and was trying to drag things out.'

'Well done, you, then,' Gian said, and then sighed because he did not need Ariana under his precious roof, and the drama that would undoubtedly entail. 'Why here, Ariana? Why La Fiordelise, Rome?'

'Because I love it,' she admitted. She looked up at the high ceilings and the gilded mirrors and the beauty that never failed to capture her heart. There was a sense of peace and calm that Gian had created, a haven that somehow made her feel safe. 'I am sure your other hotels are stunning—in fact, I have stayed in the London one several times—it is just...' She tried her best to explain it. 'There is so much history here, so much...' She faltered and then pushed on. 'It was your great-great-grandfather's?' she checked.

'You will learn the history in your induction.'

'Can you at least give me the condensed version?' Ariana asked, running a hand along a marble column and frowning at an indentation, a mar in perfection.

'That is a bullet hole,' Gian told her, 'from when the hotel became a fortress in the Second World War.'

She breathed in, shivering at the history and aching, actually aching, to know more. But Gian was glancing beyond her shoulder now, and Ariana sensed she was running out of her allotted time. 'Can I see the penthouse suite? The original one?'

'No.'

'Please.'

God, Gian thought, she was incessant. 'There might be guests.'

'I'm sure you would know.'

He sighed. 'You are most persistent.' He took out his phone and though he knew there were no guests due in the most expensive suite until tomorrow, he double-checked just to be sure, and almost sighed when he saw that indeed it was vacant. 'Very well, but only briefly.'

As they took the elevator up, Ariana had a question. 'Is your apartment on the penthouse floor?'

'No, though it is where I grew up,' Gian told her, 'but when I took over La Fiordelise, I decided I could not afford the luxury of misappropriating the hotel's most valuable asset.'

As well as that, the penthouse floor had been the loneliest place in the world for Gian. He would sometimes glimpse his parents drifting off to some event, or hear first the laughter and merriment of parties, and then lie drenched in dread as the gathering flared and got out of hand.

But as dark as his memories were, the penthouse floor was an asset indeed. This was confirmed by her gasp as she stepped into the main suite.

Rome was spread out before them and from this vantage she looked down at the square and across to Palazzo Pamphili, where her brother's wedding would be held, but that was not all that held her gaze. She wandered the vast space, taking in the ornaments and oil paintings that surely belonged behind a rope in a gallery and yet they were there for the luckiest guests to take in at their leisure.

'This corridor can be closed off,' Gian explained as she peered into the spare bedrooms, each as exquisite as the next; there was even a gorgeous library that had a huge fire, just waiting to be lit.

And then he showed her the master suite and it felt as if she wasn't just in Rome but was at the very centre of it. The bed was draped in gold, the intricately painted ceilings a masterpiece of their own, and it was as if the walls had their own pulse. Ariana was rich, but there was, of course, a pecking order, and the Penthouse Suite was not Ariana's domain. 'Is this where my parents would stay for the Romano Ball?'

Her question went unanswered, for Gian never commented on the sleeping arrangements of his guests and anyway, her eyes would fall out if he told her the truth.

'And now Dante?' she persisted.

Still he said nothing, and it was Ariana who filled the gap. 'I could live here for ever,' she sighed, sinking onto a plump lounge and kicking off her stilettoes.

'Believe me...' Gian started, but did not finish.

Certainly, he would not be sharing with Ariana that he loathed coming up here. There were just too many memories that resided here. Instead, he pointed out another of its disadvantages. 'It takes for ever to clean, which you might soon find out,' Gian said with a wry edge, and he watched as she tucked her slender legs under her. 'A full two days to service properly.'

'Let me dream for a moment,' she sighed. 'So this was built for the Duke's mistress?'

'Incorrect.'

'Correct me then,' Ariana said, her voice dropping to huskiness as, for the first time in her life, she officially flirted. Not that Gian even noticed, for he proceeded to give her a history lesson.

'It was officially built for the Duke and the Duchess,' Gian told her. 'It was actually first called La Duchessa,' Gian said, 'well, officially, but the locals all called it La Fiordelise...'

She watched as he pulled back some ornate panelling to reveal a heavy door and in it a silver key. 'Fiordelise lived through here.'

He turned the key and pushed open the door to reveal another completely separate penthouse suite, in feminine reds and with a view of the square and a personality of its own. Yet he was somewhat surprised when the rather nosy Ariana did not untangle her long legs and pad over to look at the sumptuous boudoir. Instead she screwed up her nose. 'The poor Duchess.' Her sloe eyes narrowed. 'How awful to live with just a wall between you and your husband's mistress.'

'You don't find the story of La Fiordelise romantic?'

'History makes it *appear* romantic.' Ariana shrugged. 'I find it offensive.'

Of course, given her father's *supposed* affair with Mia, he guessed that infidelity would be one of her hot buttons, but he sensed that her thoughts had been formed long ago. There was a side to Ariana he had never seen: a free thinker was in there, though somewhat suppressed.

'Why do you find it so offensive?' Gian asked. 'Things were very different back then.'

'I doubt *feelings* were different,' Ariana said. 'And I hate it that the Duchess had to vie for his attention. You would hope, once married, all that would stop.'

'All what?'

'Being shut out. It should have been the Duchess on his mind, not Fiordelise.'

Gian looked at her thoughtfully. 'You have a very idealistic view of marriage.'

'Absolutely I do,' Ariana agreed. She stood and padded over to where Fiordelise had once resided and, standing in the doorway with him, peered into the opulent, sensual, feminine suite. Yet she did not set as much as a foot inside, just faced him in the doorway. 'And that is why I am still single.'

His eyes never left her face as she continued to speak. 'My mother has spent the last quarter of a century planning my wedding—any old billionaire will do—but I shall only marry for love.' She smiled at him then and teased him a little. 'Do you even know what that word means, Gian?'

'No,' he replied, 'and I don't care to find out.'

'As is your prerogative, but it is mine to feel sad for the Duchess. What was her name?'

'Violetta,' Gian answered, 'like...' He hesitated, for he had been about to compare the name to Ariana's eyes. For several reasons, that would not be a sensible thing to do. Neither was the way he was looking into them right now.

Yes, he had noticed the huskiness of her voice and the earlier batting of her eyelashes. There was a friction in the Ariana-scented air, and his hand wanted to know for itself the softness of her cheek—so much so that Gian had to focus on not lifting his hand and cupping her face.

Gian, despite his formidable reputation, had scruples, and to kiss her, as he now desired to, while still involved with Svetlana was not something he would do.

And, aside from that, this was Ariana Romano.

The daughter of a man he respected and the little sister of his lifelong friend. And soon to be an employee. A casual affair she could never be, and that was all Gian wanted or knew.

Ariana Romano was completely off limits.

CHAPTER FOUR

'Violetta.' Ariana repeated the name of the forgotten Duchess while gazing into his eyes. 'That's beautiful.'

She practically handed him a response—*and so are you*—except Gian refused to rise to the bait.

Or rather he fought not to rise.

They stood facing each other in the doorway, their bodies almost as close as when they danced their one duty dance each year at the Romano Foundation Ball.

And he was as turned on as he had been while holding her in that dress of silver.

Of course it had been more than an educated guess, for she had looked utterly stunning that night.

Gian was well aware of his past with women.

And he was decided on his future too.

Casual, temporary, fleeting, there were many ways to describe the nature of his relationships, except entering into any of the above with Ariana was an impossible concept. If they were seen out more than a couple of times the press would soon get hold of it and her mother would too. As much as Angela resented Gian for holding Rafael's second wedding here, she would forgive him in an instant to have a title in the family.

No, there could be no kisses, though certainly the moment was ripe for one...

'What?' Ariana said. She could feel a sudden charge in the air, a slight frisson that had her on her guard. She assumed he was displeased and wondered if perhaps she shouldn't have brought up the Duchess's name, or been so derisive of Fiordelise.

Ariana could not read men.

Well, not real men, which Gian undoubtedly was.

She could read fake men, who wanted to be seen with her just for appearances' sake. And though she tried to convince herself they cared, she could never bring herself to take it beyond anything other than a tasteless kiss.

Despite popular gossip, Ariana was completely untouched.

Her flirting was all for the cameras.

No, she could not read *this* man, who stared into her eyes and gritted his jaw and, in the absence of experience, she assumed he was displeased.

'I've offended you,' Ariana said. Completely misreading the tension, she shrugged, not caring in the least if she had upset him by refusing to rave about the mistress, Fiordelise.

'You haven't offended me,' Gian said, snapping back into business mode. 'I'm just telling you the history of the place—as you asked.'

'Well, I've enjoyed hearing it.'

It was nice to be here with Gian.

Nice to have a conversation that was about more than the latest fashion or who was sleeping with whom.

It was, quite simply, nice.

'Tell me more,' Ariana said, walking back through to the master bedroom and resuming her place on the lounge. Bending over, she pulled on one of her suede stilettoes.

'There's not much more to tell.'

'Liar.' She smiled and caught his eye. 'Go on,' she persisted, 'tell me something that no one else knows.'

'Why would I do that?'

'Why wouldn't you?' she asked, peering up at him through her eyelashes as she wedged the other shoe on.

Usually, Gian could not wait to get out of the Penthouse Suite, yet Ariana was so curious and the company so pleasing that he decided the world could surely wait and he told her a titbit that very few knew. 'The Duke had a ring made for Fiordelise.'

'A ring?' That got her interest and Gian watched as her pupils dilated at the speed of a cat's. 'What was it like?'

'It is the insignia of the hotel,' Gian told her. 'The Duke would only ever let her look at it, though; she never once put it on. He held onto it on the promise that one day he would marry her.'

'I'm liking the Duke less and less,' Ariana said, smiling.

'Then you'll be pleased to know that when the Duchess died and he offered Fiordelise the ring, she declined it.'

'Really?'

'Yes. By then she had fallen in love with a servant. The old Duke was too tired to be angry, and too embarrassed by her rejection to ever admit the truth. Fiordelise saw out her days in her boudoir with her manservant tending to her needs...'

'Good for her.' Ariana smirked.

'Don't tell the guests, though.'

She laughed, and it sounded like a chandelier had caught the wind.

Right there, in the presidential suite of his signature hotel, something shifted for Gian.

Ariana was more than beautiful.

And she was more complex than he had known.

More, he admired her for the mutinous act of

trying to shed her pampered existence—with conditions of course. 'Come on,' he said, trying to keep the reluctance from his tone as they left the vast and luxurious cocoon of the suite.

'What's down there?' Ariana asked as they came out into the corridor and she saw that there was a door on the other side. 'Is there *another* penthouse suite?'

'No, there's a butler's room and kitchen and some storage space…' His expression was grim as she wandered off to explore. What was now the butler's room had been home for his many nannies. 'What's this one for?' she asked, and peered into a dour windowless room, unaware it was where Gian had slept as a child. There were shelves holding spare laptops, computer screens, chargers, adaptors, magnifying mirrors, straightening irons, and anything else a guest might have forgotten or need. 'Miscellaneous items.' Ariana concluded.

'Precisely.'

Oh, that frisson was back, only it felt different this time, and Ariana was quite sure that this time he really was displeased so she closed the door on the windowless room.

They were soon in the elevator. That clinging scent she wore was reaching him again, and he turned rather harshly towards her. 'If you do commence work at La Fiordelise you should know that perfume is banned for staff. It is not pleasant for the guests as some have allergies.'

'*You* wear cologne,' Ariana rather belligerently pointed out, for those citrus and bergamot notes had long been the signature of his greeting and the scent she breathed once a year when they danced.

'Yes, but I am not servicing the rooms. Please remember not to wear perfume for work.'

'I don't wear perfume.'

'Oh, please.'

'But I don't.' Ariana frowned. 'My skin is too sensitive.'

He wanted to debate it, to point out that the small elevator smelt of sunshine and rain and an undernote that he could not define, but the doors opened and he stepped out to the relative neutrality of Reception. He would have a word with Vanda, Gian decided. She could talk to her about perfume and such, because policing Ariana would no doubt be a full-time job! 'Are you sure you aren't just coveting the suit and pearls that my guest services managers wear?' Gian checked, as Bianca, one of his senior staff, smiled a greeting as she passed.

'Of course, not.' Ariana shook her head and flushed at her own lie, because the gorgeous blush tartan outfits were divine. 'I'm not that shallow. I really want this, Gian.'

'Well, I mean it, Ariana. If you blow this, I shall not be giving you another chance. You are to be here at seven on Monday morning,' Gian said. 'If you're late, if you're ill, if your arm is hanging off, I still don't want to hear it. Any problems, any issues, any *excuses* are no longer my concern. Vanda shall deal with you.'

And no doubt Vanda would soon fire her. 'I will say goodbye to you here,' he said.

'I need to collect my bag from your office.'

Of course she did!

He tried not to notice the feeling of the sun stepping into his office again as they walked in. 'Thank you for the tour.' Ariana smiled, 'I absolutely loved hearing about the Duke and Duchess, and Fiordelise, even if I do not approve. I'm glad she never got to wear the ring.'

He should conclude the meeting. They were already running over her unallotted time and Svetlana was waiting impatiently in the Pianoforte Bar, yet such was her enthusiasm, so unexpected the brightness of her company that instead of dismissing her Gian headed to the safe hidden in his wall.

He rarely opened the safe. In it were documents and rolls of plans, and there were also the coroner's and police reports from the deaths of his parents and brother, but there was also one thing of beauty nestled atop them.

'Come here,' Gian told her.

Those words sent an unfamiliar shiver through her, so unfamiliar that Ariana did not ask why, or what for. Instead, she followed his command and walked over.

He removed a faded velvet box from the safe. It might once have been gold, but it had faded now to a silver beige, yet it was beautiful still. The box was studded with gold tacks and the clasp was so intricate that she wondered how he flicked it open so easily.

'Look,' Gian said.

Fiordelise's ring was the rarest of treasures. It was a swirl of stunning Italian rose gold, and in the centre was a ruby so deep and so vibrant it made her breath hitch.

'I've never seen a ruby of that colour,' Ariana breathed. 'It's the colour of a pomegranate kernel, although it's bigger...'

'It's called pigeon-blood red,' Gian corrected. 'The colour of the first drops after a kill.'

'Don't.' Ariana shuddered. 'I like pomegranate better.'

'Then pomegranate red it is.' Gian smiled and then closed up the box. 'I found this five years after I inherited the place.'

'Where did you find it?'

'Under the very spot you were seated a short while ago,' Gian told her. 'When the suite was being renovated they pulled up the floor. There was a hidden basement and in it was a box. There was a shawl and some sketches of Fiordelise, and also this…'

'What happened to the sketches?' Ariana asked.

'I had them restored and framed.'

'And the shawl?'

'I gave that to an aunt. But this…' He replaced the box in the safe. 'God alone knows it would have been easier to have found this some five years earlier.'

'You'd have sold it?' Ariana frowned. She knew that he had inherited his estate from his family in the direst of conditions, and that La Fiordelise had been on the brink of collapse, yet she could not believe he would have sold something as precious and sentimental as this ring.

But Gian was adamant. 'Absolutely I would have.'

'I don't believe you.'

'Then you don't know me,' Gian said, closing up the safe. He turned to her. 'I shall have Luna bring your coat.'

'Thank you,' Ariana said, trying to quash the thud of disappointment that he hadn't suggested, given the hour, that they have dinner together. Well, she would soon see about that. 'Gosh, it's almost seven!' Ariana exclaimed. 'No wonder I'm so hungry.'

'Indeed,' Gian said. 'I should let you get on.'

She tried to stall him again. 'What about my uniform? Don't I need to be measured?'

'You'll be working as a chambermaid for the first few weeks of your rotation. That uniform comes in small, medium or large, I believe.'

There was the tiniest wrinkle of her pretty nose and then she shrugged. 'I lied,' Ariana admitted. 'I do want the tartan and pearls.'

'I know you do.'

'And I *shall* get them one day. I shall be the best guest services manager you've ever had.' She pictured her pretty pink business cards with her name embossed in rose gold: *Ariana Romano, VIP Guest Services Manager.*

Perhaps she shouldn't be so vocal with her dreams, but when she looked up she was startled by the glimmer of a smile softening his mouth.

It was a smile she had never seen on him before.

Ariana had known him for a long time. If there was trouble in her life—and all too often there was—it was Gian she ran to. And when, inevitably, she thanked him for sorting whatever problem she had placed in his lap, he would nod and give her his grim, somewhat weary smile. There was another smile she knew: each year they sat side by side at the Romano Ball, and each year he performed a duty dance, and so of course she was privy to his duty smile.

Yes, his duty smile, she called it, for that was exactly what it was.

She saw it used on guests, on dignitaries and on herself as recently as this evening when she had first walked in. *This* smile, though, was different. This *off-duty* smile felt as if it was just for her, though it was fading now and his grey eyes returned to guarded.

'I really do need to get on,' Gian said as Luna appeared with her coat.

As she and Gian walked out, Ariana saw the stunning woman from the Pianoforte Bar smile over at him. 'I'll be with you in just a moment.' Gian nodded to her and from the lack of affection in his tone she assumed he had another client.

'I thought I was your last appointment,' Ariana said.

'You were.'

He stalked off then to the waiting woman, who lifted her face to him, clearly expecting a most thorough kiss, but instead Ariana heard his slight rebuke. 'I said I would meet you at the theatre, Svetlana.'

'I thought we might have dinner in the restaurant,' Svetlana purred and needlessly fiddled with the lapel of his jacket. 'You still haven't taken me there.'

Oh!

Ariana's face was on fire, yet she could not

look away. It was unsettling to see him with a woman when of course it should not be, given his reputation. It just felt different seeing it first-hand and flicked a little knife toward her heart.

'Maybe after...?' Svetlana persisted.

Gian was not enamoured of women who purred, or those who felt the need to pick an imaginary piece of lint from his lapel, and Svetlana had been doing a lot of both of those of late.

He had already decided they were over, and was about to tell Svetlana, but with Ariana so close, for reasons he did not care—or dare—to examine, he chose not to. 'Come,' he said, 'we'll be late.'

He didn't even glance in Ariana's direction as he headed off. After all, if he stopped to say goodbye to each member of staff, he would never get out of the door.

Ariana Romano as staff?

Ariana in his hotel each and every day...

Instantly, he regretted his decision to take her on.

But then, on Monday morning, an hour after Ariana *should have* commenced her first shift, he received a text.

Gian, I am sorry! There has been an Extraordinary Board Meeting called!!!! Can I start in the afternoon instead?

Very deliberately, Gian didn't respond.

He didn't even scold her for her excessive use of exclamation marks; after all, Ariana personified them. This could never, ever work, and when she came in, hours late, on her very first day, Gian would tell her exactly why.

At lunchtime, rather than text she called him, no doubt with yet more excuses.

'Gian—'

'I don't want to hear it,' Gian cut in abruptly. 'Ariana, I simply do not want to know. Even after I gave explicit instructions not to do so, you still think you can call and text me with excuses for why you're late or not coming in. I don't deal with junior—'

'Gian, please, just listen to me...'

She was starting to cry, but Gian was way too used to her crocodile tears. 'I knew on Friday you were unsuitable for the role and your behaviour today merely confirms it. This could never have worked.'

'Gian...' she sobbed, but though he refused to be moved his mask slipped and he forgot to be polite. 'You sat in this office and pleaded for a start, and I gave you one. The contracts were drawn up and waiting to be signed, but clearly something more enticing has come along. I don't want to hear about extraordinary board meetings. The only extraordinary thing was that I actually thought you had changed your precocious, self-serving ways, but clearly you have not.'

Problem solved, Gian thought as he terminated the call. He was a little breathless, and barely holding onto his temper but he also felt a strange disappointment that, yet again, Ariana had let herself down. She was incapable of seeing things through. She was absolutely devoid of any sense of responsibility. She was always onto the next best thing the second it showed up.

Yet there was a mounting sense of disquiet to have heard her tears, for there had been an unfamiliar rasp to them that had, on reflection, sounded real.

She'd probably been putting it on, Gian told himself. If Ariana really wanted a career then perhaps she should have considered acting.

The ridiculous thing was, as he sat there, he was envisioning her in the blush pink tartan suit and the string of pearls that she had admitted she secretly desired.

Ariana, whether he wanted her to or not, made him smile, and for Gian that was rare indeed.

His private phone was buzzing and he saw that it was Dante who was calling, no doubt hoping to sway Gian from his decision.

'Pronto,' Gian said.

There was silence for a moment.

'Dante?' Gian checked. 'Look, if you're calling to excuse Ariana and ask—'

'Gian,' Dante interrupted. 'I don't know what you're referring to. I just wanted to call you before word got out. I'm sorry to have to tell you, but a short while ago my father…' Dante cleared his throat. 'Rafael has passed away.'

CHAPTER FIVE

GIAN DE LUCA MIGHT BE the last Duke of Luctano, but to him Rafael Romano had always been King.

In modern times, Rafael Romano had put Luctano on the map far more than the De Lucas, who had long ago sold off their land and moved to Rome.

This cold grey morning he flew in to bid farewell to a man Gian considered not just a brilliant business mind but a man he had been proud to call a friend.

The landscape beneath his navy helicopter was familiar. A lattice of bare vines weaved across the hills and down into the valley but, deep in winter, the poppy fields were bare and silver with ice. The lake, beside which Rafael was to be buried, was at first a black, uninviting mirror, but now rippled as his helicopter neared its location.

It was to be a private burial, for Rafael's wife

and children only, and Gian was there just for the church service.

The family would now all be at the house, and though Dante had invited him to have his pilot land there, without Rafael, Gian felt he would be invading on this solemn day.

A driver had been arranged to meet him and as he took the steps down from the helicopter Gian felt a blast of bitterly cold air: the weather in Luctano was always more extreme than in Rome. He wore a long black wool coat over his tailored black suit. His thick black hair had not quite been due for a trim, but his barber had come to his apartment that morning to ensure a perfect cut and he was particularly close shaven.

With good reason.

As a car took him to the church, he recalled Rafael's words from long ago. 'Look immaculate,' Rafael had once told him. 'You are not a university student any more but the owner-manager of a five-star hotel. Get your hair cut, and for God's sake, shave.' His advice had not ended there. 'See a tailor, buy fine shoes...'

At the age of twenty, Gian had been studying architecture and living in the residences, having turned his back on his family two years previously. His scholarship had covered accommodation and his bar work funded books and food, but barely stretched to a haircut, let alone designer clothes. 'I can't afford to,' a proud Gian had dared to admit.

'You can't afford not to. Now, listen to me, it is imperative that you look the part...'

But Gian had held firm. After the tragic death of his family, he'd discovered the financial chaos his parents had left behind and the many jobs that depended on him. 'No, the accounts are a disaster. Before the fancy suits, first the staff are to be paid.'

'It doesn't work like that.'

Rafael had taken a reluctant Gian to Via dei Condotti—a fashionable street in Rome—where he had met with artisan tailors and been fitted for bespoke Italian shoes in the only true hand-out that Gian had ever received. But better than the trip had been the glimpse of having if not a father then a mentor to advise him.

The day had ended at a Middle Eastern barbershop, with hot towels and a close shave. Rafael continued with the sage advice: 'You need to attract only the best clients.'

'How, though?' Gian had asked, staring at his groomed reflection and barely recognising himself. 'La Fiordelise's reputation is in tatters and the building is in disrepair.' Gian loathed the destruction of history—how there were only a few decent areas remaining in the once elegant building. The rest was cordoned off and for the most part the hotel was faded and unkempt.

But Rafael remained upbeat. 'La Fiordelise has survived worse. It has a new owner now and its reputation will recover: all we need is a plan.'

A couple of weeks later they had contrived one.

A plan that, to this day, few knew about.

Yes, Rafael Romano had been far more of a father to Gian than his own, and Gian would miss him very much indeed.

Arriving at the church, he could feel eyes on him as the absent Duke made a rare return. Gian declined the offer of being guided to a pew and instead stood at the back of the small church and did his level best to keep from recalling the last time he'd been here—at his own family's funeral. He pondered his handling of Ariana when she had tried to tell him her father had died. Of course he had tried to call her back and apologise, but had been sent straight to voicemail...

Gian's words, though, had been an unwitting lifeline.

It was Gian's deep, calm voice on this terrible morning that brought Ariana a little solace.

'Ariana,' Dante snapped as they all stood in the entrance hall of their father's home, preparing to head out for the funeral procession. It was

exquisitely awkward as of course it was Mia's
home too. Her older brother was in a particularly
picky mood. 'Surely you can get off your phone
for five minutes?'

But Ariana ignored him as she listened again
to Gian's message.

*'I should have let you speak. Ariana, I apolo-
gise and I am so deeply sorry for your loss. Call
me if you want to, if not...'* His deep voice halted
for a few seconds. *'You will get through this, Ariana. You are strong. Remember that.'*

Ariana didn't feel very strong, though.

She was weak from having to comfort her
mother through the day, and at night, though
exhausted, she could barely sleep. She felt as if
she were holding a million balls in the air and
that at any moment one might drop, for her family, scattered by Mia's presence, had not been
under one roof since the divorce, let alone the
roof of a church.

Surely her mother would not create a scene?

Or her aunts or uncles…

As well as the worry of that, as she headed out
to the waiting cars, the loneliest morning of her
life felt even more desolate when Dante decided
to take a seat in the front vehicle with Mia, rather
than make her travel to the church by herself.
That left Ariana with Stefano and Eloa, which
lately felt like the equivalent of being alone.

As the cortège moved through the hills to the village, Ariana tried to come to grips with a world without her father while acknowledging a disquieting truth.

Since her father had found Mia, he too had pushed her aside.

For two years, she had felt like a visitor in the family home and later at his hospital bedside. Perhaps she could have accepted Mia more readily if they had accepted her more into their world. Yes, she regretted now not going to the wedding, but the truth was her father hadn't exactly pushed for her to attend.

In fact, he'd seemed a touch relieved when Ariana had declined.

Once she had been the apple of her father's eye and they would talk and laugh. They would fly to the London office together, and she had felt there was a real place for her on the Romano board, but since Dante had taken over all she had felt was supernumerary.

Ariana didn't just miss her father today; she had missed him for the last two years of his life. And now she would miss him for ever, with no time left to put things to rights.

'We're here,' Eloa announced, breaking into her thoughts, and Ariana looked up and saw they were at the church.

The doors were opened and the trio stepped

out. Her legs felt as if they had been spun in brittle steel wool, and might snap as she walked over the cobbles and into the church. Her heart felt like a fish flopping in her chest that might jump out of her throat if she let out the wail she held in. The sight of her father's coffin at the front of the church, though expected, was so confronting that she wanted to turn around and flee, unsure whether she was capable of getting through the ceremony.

But then, just as she felt like panic would surely take over, came an unexpected moment of solace.

Gian was here.

Of course he was, but it was the actual *sight* of him, the glimpse of him, that allowed Ariana to draw a deeper breath.

He looked more polished and immaculate than she had ever seen; his black hair was brushed back from his face and she could see both the compassion and authority in his grey eyes.

Yes, authority, for him standing at the back with a full view of proceedings instantly calmed Ariana.

Gian would not let things get out of hand.

He would keep things under control.

And then she knew that it wasn't the hotel, or the haven in Rome that Gian had created, that calmed her.

It was Gian himself who made the world safe.

The look they shared lasted less than a moment—Gian gave her a small, grim smile of sympathy, a nod of his noble head, more by way of understanding than greeting—but time had taken on a different meaning, for the velvet of his eyes and the quiet comfort they gave would sustain her through the service.

You are strong.

He had told her so.

And so she did her best to get through the eulogy and the hymns and the hell.

Gian had been through this before, Ariana reminded herself as she did her level best not to stare at the coffin.

There had been three coffins in this church when his family had died. Pink peonies on his mother's, white lilies on his father's and a huge spray of red poppies on his brother's.

'I don't like this, Papà,' she had whispered, for she'd been ten years old and the chants and scent of incense had made her feel a little ill.

'I know, bella, but we are here today for Gian,' her *papà* had said.

'Shouldn't we sit with him, then?' Ariana had asked, for even beside his aunts and such he had looked so completely alone.

'We are not family,' her *papà* had said. *'Hold my hand.'*

His warm hand had closed around hers and imbued her with strength, but she had looked over at Gian and seen that there was no one holding his.

And there was no one holding Ariana's today.

It was an emotional service, but Gian refused to let it move him and stood dry-eyed even as the coffin was carried out to the haunting strains of his favourite aria—Puccini's 'O Mio Babbino Caro'. *Oh, my dear Papà...*

Ariana looked close to fainting, but her damned mother was too busy beating at her chest to see.

'Hey,' Gian said. To the frowns of the congregation, he broke protocol and joined the family on the way out. 'You are doing so well,' he murmured quietly.

'I am not.'

'You are, you are.' He could feel her tremble. As the family lined up outside the church, instead of guiding her to join them, he took Ariana aside and held her.

She leaned on him for a moment, a blissful moment that smelt of Gian, and she learned something more about him. There were no tears in his eyes, he looked a little pale but unmoved, yet his heart beat rapidly in his chest and she could *feel* his grief as he held her in his arms.

As they held each other.

'You'll miss him too,' she whispered.

'Ever so.'

It was the closest she had ever been to him, this blissful place on a terrible day, and she wanted to cling on, to rest in his arms a while longer, but he was pulling her back and returning to his usual distant form.

'Gian.' It was so cold to stand without him, especially when she wanted the shield of his arms. 'I don't think I can face the burial.'

'Yes, Ariana, you can.'

But hysteria was mounting. 'No. I really don't think so...'

'Would it help if I came with you?'

It would, but... 'You can't.' She gave a black laugh. 'Stefano practically had to put in a written request to Dante to have Eloa attend, and she's his fiancée. Mamma has been denied. God, Gian, I don't...'

'Take this.'

From deep in his coat pocket he handed her a *cornicello*...a small gold amulet. 'Your father gave me this to hold when I buried my family. You *can* do this, Ariana; you will regret it if you don't.'

It was the most private of burials.

Mia, who could barely stand, held a single lily.

And Dante, who loathed Mia possibly the most

of all Rafael's children, was the one who had to take her to the graveside so she could throw the flower in.

Stefano wept and was comforted by Eloa, and that left Ariana standing alone, holding onto the little sliver of gold.

Ariana had never felt so cold as when she returned to the house and stood by a huge fire, grateful for the large cognac someone placed in her hands. Looking up, she saw it was Gian. 'Thank you.'

'How was it?' Gian gently enquired.

'It is done,' Ariana responded, without really answering and then held out the amulet. 'Here, I should give this back to you. Thank you.'

'Keep it.'

'He gave it to you,' Ariana said, suddenly angry at his lack of sentiment. This man who would sell a priceless ring, this man who would let go of a gift from her father. 'Why would you give it away?'

'Did it help?' he asked, and she nodded. 'Then you yourself might pass it on someday when someone else needs your father's strength.'

Never, she thought.

Never, ever.

For it was her first gift from Gian and it almost scared her how much that meant.

'It seems strange to be here without him,' Gian

admitted, trying to gauge how she felt, but for once the effusive Ariana was a closed book. She gave a tired shrug and her black lashes closed on violet eyes highlighting the dark shadows beneath them.

'It has felt strange to be here for quite some time.' Her eyes opened then and came to rest on Rafael's widow, and Gian followed her gaze as she spoke. 'My father and I used to be so close.'

'You were always close,' Gian refuted.

'No.' She shook her head. 'It fell away at the end.'

He would like to take her arm and walk her away from the funeral crowd, to walk in the grounds and gently tell her the difficult truth—the real reason her father had pulled away from his family and from the daughter he had loved so very much.

It was not his place to do so, though.

Oh, today he loathed being the keeper of secrets, for the truth would surely help her to heal.

'How long are you here for?' Ariana asked, determinedly changing the subject, then wishing she hadn't for the answer was not one she liked.

'I'll be leaving shortly. I just wanted to see the house one last time and…' He hesitated but then admitted the deeper truth. 'To see how you were after the burial.'

Stay longer, she wanted to say, yet she dared not.

'And,' he added, 'I wanted to properly apologise for how I spoke to you on the day you called. I was completely out of line.'

'Not completely,' Ariana said, and he watched her strained lips part into a brief glimpse of her impish smile. 'Not to come in because of a board meeting *was* inexcusable on my first day...'

'Oh!' Her burst of honesty and the explanation surprised him. 'I thought you must have had word that your father was ill.'

'No, no,' she said. 'That wasn't till later.'

'Well, even so, I'm very sorry for the way I spoke to you.'

'It's fine,' Ariana said. 'I would have been annoyed with me too.'

He watched the dart of anxiety in her eyes as he looked around the room, filled with low murmurs of conversation and her veiled *mamma*, sitting weeping on a chair against the wall surrounded by aunts. 'Mamma and Mia have never been under the same roof...'

'Everyone is behaving,' Gian pointed out.

'For now they are,' Ariana said, and let out a nervous breath, unsure how long the civility might last. 'There is the reading of the will soon.'

'It will be fine,' Gian assured her, though he quietly thought Ariana's concerns might be merited and she didn't even know the half of it! Roberto, the family lawyer, had also been Rafael's long-term lover and he was reading the will. With the current wife and widow in the room, one could be forgiven for expecting fireworks.

'Do you want me to stay until afterwards?' he offered.

'I would like that,' Ariana admitted. She looked up at the man she always ran to, always turned to, yet the moment was broken by the sound of her mother's voice.

'Gian, I was hoping that you'd come back to the house...' She placed an overly familiar hand on his arm, and Gian would have liked to shrug it off. He loathed the sudden fake friendliness from Angela, although of course it was for a reason. 'Could I ask you to take me back to Rome with you? I simply cannot stand to be here.'

'It would be my pleasure,' Gian politely agreed, for even if he did not particularly want Angela's company, he would do the right thing.

'I have to stay for the reading of the will,' Angela explained, 'but if we could leave after that? Ariana will be coming with us also...'

'But, Mamma, Stefano and Eloa are heading back to Zio Luigi's...' Ariana started, but clearly her desires had no importance here and Gian watched her shoulders slump as she acquiesced. 'If that is what you want.'

Naturally, Gian did not enter the study for the reading of the will. Instead, he poured himself a brandy from Rafael's decanter, as his friend had often done for him, and silently toasted his portrait.

What a mess.

He looked at the portrait and wondered if Rafael's truth would be revealed in the will.

Of course Angela had long since known the truth about her husband, and had fought like a cat to prevent it getting out, more than happy to let the blame for the end of their marriage land on Mia.

He looked at the pictures above the fireplace— family shots. There was a surge that felt almost like a sob building when he saw his own image there, for he had never considered he might appear on anyone's mantelpiece. Certainly there had been no images of him at his childhood home.

Yet here he was, fourteen or fifteen years old, on horseback, with Dante.

Good times.

Not great times, of course, because the end of the holidays had always meant it would be time to head back to Rome and his chaotic existence there.

The door of the study opened and the subdued gathering trooped out; Gian quickly realised that Rafael's truth had not been revealed.

'How was it?' he asked Dante, who was the first to approach him.

'Fine. No real surprises.'

And then came Ariana. She looked pale and drained, as if all the exuberance and arrogance that he was coming to adore had simply been leached from her.

'How did it go?' Gian asked.

'I don't even know how to answer,' she admitted. 'I am taken care of. I have an apartment in Paris and I will never have to work.' She gave a tired shrug. 'Does that mean it went well?'

'Ariana,' he cut in, and his hand reached for her arm but she pulled it back.

Not because she didn't want physical contact, more because of how much she did. 'I should go and say my farewells.'

'Are you sure you want to come back to Rome tonight?'

'Not really.'

'Your family are all here,' Gian pointed out. 'Wouldn't it be better to spend time with them?'

'Yes, but I think Mamma needs me. She feels so out of place here.'

It was a subdued little group that flew back to Rome. Gian's car was waiting at the airport and he gave Angela's address to the driver.

'Ariana, darling,' her mother said, 'I have the most terrible headache. I think I might just head home to bed. After I've been dropped off, Gian's driver will take you home.'

'But, Mamma, I thought I was to stay with you tonight.'

Gian heard the strain in Ariana's voice. She was clearly asking to be with her mother, rather than offering to take care of her, although Angela, just as clearly, chose not to hear it as that. 'Ariana, I know you're worried about me but right now all I really need is some peace.'

Gian gritted his jaw because he could see the manipulative behaviour, pulling Ariana away from the rest of the family just because she could when she'd always intended to spend the evening with Thomas, her lover.

He knew now that he loathed Angela because she was as selfish as his own mother had been.

'I'll call you tomorrow,' Angela said to her daughter as she got out of the car. 'Thank you, Gian, for seeing us home.'

Eternally polite, usually he would have wished her well and forced himself to kiss her cheeks, but the best he could manage was a curt nod.

As the driver closed the door, he looked over at Ariana. She was staring straight ahead and there was the sparkle of unshed tears in her eyes that he knew were waiting to fall the very second she was alone. 'Let's get you home,' Gian said as the car pulled away.

'I don't want to go home.' Ariana shook her head and blinked back the tears. 'I might call Nicki.'

Ariana's friend Nicki ran rather wild and she would undoubtedly prescribe a night of drinking and clubbing as a cure for Ariana's troubled heart. 'How come Nicki wasn't at the funeral?' he asked.

'She only got back from skiing this afternoon.' Ariana scrabbled in her purse for her phone. 'She'd have come if she could.'

Gian doubted it.

Nicki liked the galas and balls, and the spoils of being Ariana's friend, but where was she now when her friend needed her most?

Gian did not quite know what to do.

If it were Stefano, or Dante, or even Angela— who he didn't even like—Gian would suggest a drink at the hotel, or a walk perhaps. Conversation or silence, whatever they chose.

But this was Ariana.

He wished he hadn't noticed her beauty, or the colour of her eyes.

Gian wished he could snap his fingers and return them to a time when she had been just the annoying little sister of a friend, the daughter of his beloved mentor... That thought had him stepping up to do the right thing, for he did not want Ariana in questionable company tonight.

'Would you like to come back to La Fiordelise for a drink, or something to eat perhaps?'

'I...' His offer was so unexpected. Gian usually made her feel like an annoying presence, always trying to cut short their time together, and now it was he who was offering to extend it. 'I don't want to impose.'

'It doesn't normally stop you...' Gian teased, but then, seeing her frown, realised that even the lightest joke wasn't registering. 'It would be my pleasure,' he said. 'I just need to make a quick call.'

Ariana pretended not to listen as he cancelled his date for the night. And his date for the night did not take it well.

'Svetlana,' he said, and Ariana blinked at the slight warning edge to his tone as she looked out at the dark streets. 'Not now.'

And that slight warning edge had her stomach clenching and a small flush rising to her cheeks. She looked at Gian, who appeared incredibly bored at the unfolding drama.

Yes, drama, for she could hear the rise in Svetlana's voice, and foolish, foolish Svetlana, Ariana thought, for she literally watched his impassiveness transform to disdain.

'Svetlana, I am unable to see you tonight,' Gian said, and then, when it was clear she had asked why, rather drily he answered, 'Because I am unable to see you tonight.'

His lack of explanation must have infuriated Svetlana for even with the phone to his ear, Ariana heard her angry retort. 'When then?'

'Do I have to spell it out, Svetlana?'

It would appear that he did, and Ariana listened as very coldly and firmly he ended their relationship.

'Gian,' she said as they pulled up at La Fiordelise, 'please, call her back. I can go home. I really didn't want to make trouble for you…'

'Forget it.' He gave a dismissive shrug. 'We were always going to end.'

In fact, he hadn't seen Svetlana all week.

Somehow they had bumped through the concert at Teatro dell'Opera but instead of returning to the sumptuous suite behind his office, Gian had taken her home.

'Why did you break up with her?' Ariana asked as they stood outside the car beneath the bright entrance lights.

'Because she wanted more.'

'More?'

'She had started to drop into the hotel unannounced,' he said. Ariana just frowned. 'And she wanted to come up to my residence…'

Her frown deepened.

'As well as that, she wanted to come with me to your father's funeral.'

'Oh?' Ariana said, but it was more a question, because she didn't really understand.

'As if we were a couple.' Gian attempted to explain his closed-off life, but clearly still bewildered, Ariana gave the tiniest shake of her head and so he elaborated. 'She wanted things to progress and that was not what we had agreed.'

'What did you agree to?'

'Only the best parts.' Gian did not soften his words. 'Dinner in a nice restaurant, a trip to the theatre…'

'I assume sex?'

'Correct.'

'So if not in your residence…'

'Ariana, I am not discussing this with you. Suffice it to say I never want a relationship.' He ended the matter. 'You're cold, let's go in.'

'To the restaurant?' Ariana asked.

'I thought the Pianoforte Bar…'

Her eyes narrowed, recalling Svetlana being denied a seat at his restaurant. Despite his kind invitation to keep her company, she knew she was also being kept at arm's length.

'No, thank you.' She shook her head. 'I don't need the noise of a bar tonight, even one as elegant as yours…' Ariana fished and she fished, but Gian did not take the bait, nor upgrade her to restaurant status, even as she stood there and sulked. 'I think I might go for a walk.'

'In heels?' Gian frowned.

'I have my flats in my bag. I'll be fine on my own,' she said, waving him away as she took off her heels and went to put her flats on, but where was a marble pillar when you needed one?

Gian would not be waved off, though, and neither was he Prince Charming, for he did not go down on his knees to help, instead offering his arm. 'Lean on me.' He took one black stiletto that she handed to him and passed her a flat, and then it was all repeated with the other foot.

'Let's walk,' Gian said.

For Ariana, it felt like the right choice. Piazza Navona, the grand, elegant square overlooked by La Fiordelise, was beautifully lit. Its fountains were hypnotic and a little of the tension of the day left as they strolled.

It felt different at night.

Or rather it felt different being here with Gian.

His presence was a comforting warmth in the chilly night air and his voice felt like a welcome caress, as he enquired how things were with her brothers.

'Dante is…' Ariana let out a long sigh. 'I don't know. He's just been so focused on the funeral. I think it will all hit him afterwards. He and my father were close.'

'Yes,' Gian agreed.

'Well, they were until Mia came along.'

'They grew close again, once your father became ill,' Gian pointed out. 'And Stefano?'

'I wouldn't know,' Ariana said tightly. 'You would have to ask Eloa.' She heard the bitterness in her own voice and screwed her eyes closed, because she had told no one, not even Nicki, how left out she felt. 'Sorry, I didn't mean that.'

'Yes, you did,' Gian said gently. 'I know the two of you are close.'

'*Were* close,' she corrected. 'I know it sounds childish, but we used to speak every day. Now he calls Eloa, and that's correct, of course, and how it should be; they're getting married in May. However...' She didn't know how best to describe the loneliness that had descended almost the moment Eloa had been introduced to her and Ariana had felt shut out.

'You miss him?'

'Yes.' She nodded. 'And especially now.'

'Since your father died?'

'Before that,' Ariana admitted. She looked at the moon lighting up the square. If ever there was a time for honesty it was tonight. 'When our parents broke up it was Stefano I turned to. Papà had eyes only for Mia; he didn't want me around so much...'

Gian stayed silent, for he knew that wasn't

quite the case. Rafael had found out he was dying and wanted his final years to be spent in peace with Roberto; Mia had been a front of respectability. Of course he could not reveal that and just listened as she continued. 'But Stefano met Eloa around then,' Ariana said. 'I just felt as if everyone I was close to disappeared. I know I have Dante, but he is so much older...'

'Ancient,' Gian agreed drily, for he and Dante were the same age.

'I have Mamma, of course, but...' She wished he would interrupt, or finish her sentence for her, because it was perhaps not something she should say out loud, yet his continued silence compelled her to speak. 'I have Mamma, though only on her terms, and it can be a little stifling at times.'

Still he remained silent as they walked.

'And a little solitary at others,' Ariana admitted. 'I thought things were different with Stefano. He's my twin; I'm used to him being there and I thought, no matter what, we'd still be in each other's lives. I'm happy for him, I honestly am. I'm just not so happy for me. I'm being selfish, I know. Childish...'

'Ariana.' Gian thought for a moment and then decided he could be honest about this much at least. 'For what it's worth, I think Stefano is wrong to shut you out.'

Her head turned towards him, her eyes wide

with surprise. She'd expected to be scolded or
told she was being petty or jealous. Instead he
seemed like he was on her side. 'Really?'

'From everything I can observe, since Eloa
came along he's dropped everyone and everything. I didn't realise until today that that also
extended to you. Don't you and Eloa get on?'

'That's the ridiculous part,' Ariana said, relieved to speak about something other than
death, and also relieved to share what had been
eating at her for months. 'I like Eloa, I really do.
They just don't seem to want to spend any real
time with me.'

'I'm sorry.'

'It doesn't matter.' She gave a tight shrug, at
first closing the conversation but then opening
it up in a way he had not anticipated. 'Were you
close to your brother...' She had to think for a
second to recall his name. 'Eduardo?'

'No,' Gian said. At first his answer was final,
but she had shared so much with him that he
felt it right to share a little more. 'We were for
a while.'

'Oh.'

'For a long while I looked up to him. Admired
him...'

'And then?'

'And then I didn't.'

He gave her no more.

'Wait there,' Gian said. She assumed he had to make a call, perhaps to Svetlana… Maybe he was bored already with the company he had chosen tonight.

Alone for the first time that day, Ariana quietly admitted her deep feelings for him.

Ariana wanted more of Gian.

She wanted to know his kiss. She wanted… more.

More than his kiss…

To know his touch…

To sit holding hands at his table…

The more she admitted to herself, the more honest her admissions became…

She wanted Gian to hold her and she wanted to know how it felt to be made love to by him.

For Gian De Luca to be her first…

It was a reckless thought, though, for by his own admission Gian came with a warning.

But since when had Ariana heeded warnings?

She stared up at Fontana dei Quattro Fiumi—the Fountain of Four Rivers, said to be the most complex of the many fountains in Rome. She looked at the four river gods and then up, ever up, to the tall obelisk that topped it. Her feelings were spinning in her mind as the crush she had on Gian transformed into need.

She loathed being twenty-five with barely a kiss to her name.

Yet while kisses did not excite her, the mere thought of Gian's kiss did.

'Here.' His voice startled her and she looked at the paper cone filled with hot chestnuts that he held out. 'You looked cold.'

'You got these for me?' Gian watched as her pale face broke into a smile, and her eyes shone as if he were handing her a purse of gold. 'Thank you.'

Hot chestnuts on a cold night had never tasted so good as they sat at the base of the fountain, biting into the salty treats. 'These are the best I have tasted,' Ariana said, every single time she ate one.

'They're just chestnuts.' Gian did not really get her enthusiasm for such a familiar winter treat. 'I used to come down here at night as a child and buy these.'

'You would sneak out?' she nudged.

'No sneaking required.'

'What do you mean?'

'Just that…' Gian said, and he looked at Ariana, quietly watching the world go by. He knew why he had not left her alone tonight. He knew better than anyone how it felt to be alone in Rome after dark, that frantic search for company, any company, that compelled you to speak to a stranger or hang out with a wayward friend, anything other than return to your room and lie there alone. 'So...' he changed the subject and looked over at the stunning Palazzo Pamphili, where the wedding was to be held '...you arranged the wedding reception.'

'I managed to secure the venue,' Ariana corrected.

'Good for you.' He smiled.

His smile was like being handed the earth.

'Come on,' he suggested, when they had finished eating, 'let's walk.'

They passed the impressive building where a few months from now the wedding would take place. It seemed so wrong that such a celebration would take place and their father would not be there.

'Are you going?' she asked, because the idea of him being there really helped. She was so out of the wedding loop she had no real idea if he'd been invited, let alone responded.

'No,' he admitted. 'It's the weekend of the opening of my Florence hotel so I shall be sending my apologies. I am sure I shan't be missed.'

You shall be missed, she wanted to say, but did not know how. 'I'm kind of dreading it,' she said, hinting a little that his presence might help.

'You'll be just fine,' Gian said assuredly, and gave her hand a squeeze, yet her fingers were cold beneath his so he held onto them as they walked.

Gian did not do hand-holding.

Ever.

Yet tonight he did.

For a second, Ariana felt as if she were walking in the Tuscan fields in the middle of summer, not sad and frozen in Rome. But then she remembered the reason for his kindness this night, and wondered how it had been for him. 'You must miss your parents...' she ventured, though immediately knew she had said the wrong thing for he dropped her hand like a hot coal.

'I didn't know them enough to miss them,' he said, but Ariana refused to be fobbed off.

'What about your brother?' she probed, but he was equally unforthcoming.

'Leave it, Ariana.'

She refused. 'How did you find out about the...?' She hesitated, unsure what to call a raging fire on a yacht in the middle of the ocean. 'The accident?' she settled for.

'Hardly an accident,' Gian retorted, and she heard a trace of bitterness to his tone. 'With the amount of alcohol and class-A drugs my family consumed, I think it could be called inevitable.'

Ariana was stunned.

She had heard whispers, of course, like little jigsaw pieces of scandal that had been gathered together over dinners and parties, but all too soon scooped up and put away. But now it was Gian himself putting the pieces together and giving her a glimpse.

'They were renewing their wedding vows?' Ariana checked.

God, she was persistent. Perhaps it was the emotion of the day, but he found that tonight he didn't mind. 'Yes. It sounds romantic, doesn't it, like the Duke and Fiordelise, but the truth is it was an excuse for a party. They renewed their vows every couple of years,' Gian said drily. 'They would fight, they would make up, they would say never again... I got off the hamster wheel and left before then. I was at university, studying architecture. I was asleep in the residences...'

'You didn't live at La Fiordelise then?'

'God, no.' He gave a hollow laugh. 'I was more than happy to leave it all behind. Luna came with the police and woke me...'

'Luna worked for your parents?'

'She was actually working her notice,' Gian said. 'They had been late again paying her and she had resigned, but after they died Luna said she would stay until things were more stable.' Gian gave her a tight smile. 'Fifteen years later, she still reminds me on occasion that she is working her notice.' He shook his head and closed the subject.

Except Ariana wanted to prise it back open. 'Tell me…'

'Tell you what?'

'How you felt when they died?'

'As I told you, I barely knew them.'

'They were your parents, your brother…'

'Just leave it,' he warned. 'Ariana, I respect your boundaries. Why can't you respect mine?'

'Because I want to know you some more…'

He kept right on walking, though a little faster than before. 'Wait…' Ariana said, and grabbed his coat to slow him down, except her hand found its way back into his. 'I'm sorry for pushing. I just wonder…' she didn't know how best to say it '…when the grief goes?'

'I can't answer that,' Gian admitted. 'I grieved for them long before they died.' He should close it there, but her hand was warm and he sensed she would walk for ever just to hear some more. 'Eduardo and I were both repulsed by their ways. He was older, the one who would look out for me when I was small, make sure my nanny was paid, that sort of thing…'

She stayed silent in the hope he would continue and her reward was great, for he revealed more.

'Then he took up their ways and I ended up looking out for him.'

Still she stayed silent but she felt the grip of

his hand tighten and it seemed like the darkness of his truth guided her through her own pain.

'I found Eduardo one morning; I thought he was dead. I couldn't rouse my parents. The hotel doctor came and for all the hell of that morning, by that evening the incident was forgotten.'

Now she spoke. 'Not by you.'

'Never by me,' Gian said. 'It happened several times again. I said to Eduardo one day, "I won't always be there to save you." And it was then that I stopped...'

'Stopped what?' Ariana asked.

'I can't answer that,' Gian admitted. 'And I'm not being evasive, I just...' He shrugged. 'Stopped.'

Ariana stopped asking, which he was grateful for, because revelations like these were hard.

He had stopped...not loving, not caring, just stopped all feelings.

Stopped hoping for change.

Stopped trying to control their chaos.

'I like order,' he admitted, and looked over at her. 'Why do you smile?'

'Because it's hardly a revelation. I know you like order, Gian.'

'You know too much,' he said, and dropped a kiss on the top of her head as they walked.

It was a tiny kiss, but when it came from Gian,

it felt as if he had just picked her up and carried her.

It felt so perfect that she actually let out a little laugh and touched her head to feel where his lips had just pressed, for her scalp tingled. 'You're crazy, Ariana,' he told her.

'A bit.'

It was unexpected bliss on the saddest of nights, to be walking on a cold Rome night, hand in hand, along Piazza d'Arecoli, their breaths blowing white in the night air. Ariana had run out of words, and she was terrified that he might drop her hand.

His hand was warm and it was so unexpected and so nice and just everything she needed tonight.

Gian too was pondering the light weight of her fingers that wrapped around his and how, on the near-empty street, when they could easily walk apart, they were strolling like this.

It was Ariana Romano.

She's a friend, he told himself.

He was simply doing what any friend would.

Except he did not have friendships of this type.

And he never confided in anyone, yet he just had.

Still holding hands, they took the stairs and there before them, ever beautiful, was the Altar of the Fatherland. Soldiers stood guarding the tomb of the unknown soldier and Ariana knew she should guard her own heart with the same attention and care.

'Oh,' she gasped as they took in the altar of the goddess of Rome.

His stomach growled and he turned her to face him. There were tired streaks of mascara, like delicate lace, smudged on her cheeks. Her mouth, rarely devoid of lipstick, was swollen from days of tears. She smiled briefly and it lit up her face for a moment. He wanted to capture it, to frame it and hold onto it—and he did so with his hands.

She felt the brush of his fingers on her cheeks and then the soft pressure as he held her face. Surely the eternal flame flared, because something lit the sky and seared her as his lips made first contact.

Just the gentlest brush at first then soft and slow and exploring.

His kiss made her slightly giddy in a way no other had. His touch was both tender and firm and she felt she could fall right now and be caught, even though his hands barely held her.

Only once did she peek. Ariana opened her eyes, while praying that she wouldn't be caught, for she did not want to break this spell. Gian's eyes were closed, though, as if savouring the most exquisite wine. He continued to hold her cheeks, so firmly now that her head could not move. He kissed her thoroughly and his lips were like velvet, his tongue so shockingly intimate it felt charged as each stroke shot volts of ecstasy to her own. His hand moved into her hair, holding the back of her head and knotting into her scalp as his tongue danced with hers.

A craving for more built in her but he pulled back. Gian looked at her wet lips and dilated pupils and the frantic, somewhat startled look and he tried to rein in his usual common sense. 'I should get you home...'

'Please,' Ariana said, but her voice was low and husky and told them both what she wanted.

Ariana's decision was made.

Gian De Luca would be her first.

Perhaps that was the reason she had held on for so long, because there was no one else who held a candle to him. No one who made her shiver, even without touching her, no one who made her mouth want to know his kiss...

'Ariana.' His voice was gruff. 'When I said home, I meant to your door.' Gian was serious. A kiss was one thing, but bedding her was out of the question. 'If we were so much as seen out together...'

'That would get them talking.' Ariana smiled as Gian clearly hated the thought. 'Mamma would have us married in a moment if she knew her virgin daughter was out with the Duke...'

Her voice trailed off, unsure how Gian would receive the news of her inexperience, but he gave a low laugh.

Ariana was not, he knew, dropping in his title; instead she was capturing her mother's thought process and agreeing with exactly how it would be if they were seen. 'Exactly. Though,' he added, 'I'm sure all mothers think their daughters are virgins.'

'But I am one.'

He almost laughed again, and then realised she wasn't laughing. He almost hauled her off him, but decided that reaction might be a bit extreme and so instead he offered her his smile.

His duty smile, which she determinedly ignored.

'Let's get you home…' Gian said.

'Yes,' Ariana agreed. 'Take me to bed.'

'Absolutely not.'

And he meant it, for he was headed down the steps. Ariana did not quite know what she'd done wrong, just that everything had changed.

'Gian.' Now she really did have to practically run to keep up with him. 'Why are you being like this? Didn't you like our kiss?'

'It was a kiss,' Gian snapped, 'not an open invitation.'

But Ariana would not relent. She had made

up her mind and was all too used to getting her own way. 'I want my first to be you.'

'Well, it won't be. If we are even as much as seen, people will talk and it will be...' He had to be cruel to be kind. 'They will turn it into something bigger than it is.'

'I know that.'

'Do you?' Gian checked. 'Do you understand that I don't do relationships? That the very last thing I want is to be involved in someone else's life?'

'You're always dating.'

'Yes.'

'So what's the difference?' Ariana frowned. 'I might be innocent in the bedroom, but I am not stupid, Gian...'

'I never said you were.'

'I'm not asking for love. I don't want lies to appease and promises that you won't keep,' Ariana said. 'I'm all too familiar with them, but I do want you to make love to me.'

'Ariana—'

'No,' she broke in, and they argued in loud Italian all the way home. 'Don't make me ashamed for admitting it. I'm twenty-five and a virgin. I don't want to be married, Gian. Do you not think my mother has endless suitors in mind for me? I can't have a casual relationship or it will be a kiss and tell. You know that...'

He looked at the spoilt, immature Ariana speaking like the woman she was.

'Surely there have been kisses…?'

'Yes,' she admitted, 'plastic kisses from plastic men, but your kiss nearly made me come.'

He laughed because she fascinated him.

Like a stunning portrait, like a song you had to pause just to go back and listen to the lyrics again.

He loved how she stated her case.

They argued all the way to the swish apartment block where she lived. 'I get that I'm not as experienced or as worldly as Svetlana…'

'Stop,' Gian said. 'Just stop right there. Why would you sign up for inevitable hurt, Ariana?' Gian asked. 'You know it'll go public, and you know your family will find out, and I know that I'll end things…'

'How?' Ariana asked. She wasn't begging or persuading, more genuinely perplexed. 'How do you know?'

'Because I never want to get too close. I date women who understand from the get-go that we'll never progress further than we did on the very first night.'

'So I would get no more than a kiss and a cone of hot chestnuts,' she teased. 'Well, rest assured, you wouldn't have to worry about dumping me, Gian. I would grow bored with you very quickly.'

He didn't smile at her joke and he would not relent, but rather than face being alone she turned off the voices in her head and tried to argue with a kiss. She put her arms around his neck and pressed her mouth to his, but there was no longer solace there for his was pressed closed and unyielding, and she sobbed as he pulled his head back.

'Go in!' he warned her.

'Please, Gian, I don't want to be lonely tonight.'

But when he remained silent, Ariana got the message. He did not want her, so she scrabbled around for her dignity. 'Thank you for seeing me to my door.'

'Get some sleep.' Gian said.

'Oh, please,' Ariana scoffed as she huffed off. 'As if that's going to happen.'

He watched her leave, and by honouring Rafael he felt like he'd failed her. 'Ariana...' Gian called out, and it troubled him how quickly she turned and was back at his side.

He would not sleep with her, no matter how much they both wanted it.

He would do the right thing by Rafael *and* Ariana.

'I'll come in, but I'm taking the sofa.' She nodded, both regret and relief flooding through her as he spoke on. 'You don't have to be alone tonight.'

CHAPTER SIX

THEY PASSED THE dozing doorman and took the elevator, although Gian stood like a security guard to the side of her, rather than like a man who had almost kissed her to orgasm.

She was all dishevelled in her head as they stepped into her apartment. 'Thankfully,' Ariana said as she closed the drapes, 'it was serviced while I was away, or we would be knee-deep in...' Her voice trailed off.

Knee-deep in what? Gian wanted to ask, for there was no real evidence of her here. He could be walking into any well-heeled woman's apartment in Rome—and Gian had walked into many—and the décor would be much the same. It was all very tasteful with plump sofas and modern prints, yet it was rather like a show home and there was barely a hint of Ariana. Even her bookshelves offered no real clues, for there were a few classics on the shelves as well as elegant coffee table books. There were at least some photos up, but even they seemed carefully chosen to show, so to speak, only her best side.

'Do you want a drink?' Ariana offered.

'No, thank you.'

Now that she had him here, Ariana didn't quite know what to do with him. It was, she thought, a bit like stealing a bear from the zoo, making it your mission to get him home and then…

'I'll show you around,' she offered, 'where you're sleeping. Given that you'd rather it wasn't with me.'

'I don't need a tour,' Gian responded. 'I will stay here.' He pointed to the sofa.

'I do have a guest room.'

'I'm not here to relax.'

'You are *such* a cold comfort.'

'Better than no comfort at all. I do have some scruples, Ariana. I am not going to make love to you on the night of your father's funeral when you are upset and not thinking straight.'

'Oh, believe me, I am thinking straight. Life is short, Gian, life is for living, for loving.'

'Then you've come to the wrong man because, as I've repeatedly said, I don't do love.'

She wanted to stamp her feet. She knew she was being a bit of a diva but she was beyond caring.

When Ariana wanted something, she wanted

it now, and when she'd made up her mind…well, it was made up.

'Can you unzip my dress, please?' Ariana lifted her hair and stood with her back to him, waiting for the teeniest indicator—a run of his finger, a lingering palm, him holding his breath—as he found the little clasp at the top of the velvet dress and undid it. Yet Gian was a master of self-control and without lingering he tugged the zip down so that her back and the lacy straps of her black bra were exposed.

'There,' he said, with all the excitement of an accountant relocating a decimal point.

She turned around and her dress slipped down, exposing her shoulders and décolletage, but he looked straight into her glittering eyes and smothered a yawn. 'It's been a long day,' Gian said. 'Perhaps you should go to bed.'

'So much for the playboy of Rome,' she sneered as she headed for her room, embarrassed that he clearly did not want her.

No wonder, Ariana thought as she stood in the bathroom and looked at her blotchy tear-streaked face.

She cleansed her skin and then ran a brush listlessly through her hair. She pulled on some shorts and a T-shirt and then climbed into bed. Sulking, she pulled the covers up to her chin.

'Do you want milk or something?' Gian called.

'I'm not ten!' she shouted through the darkness. It was worse having him here like this than being alone. Except, as she lay in the dark, Ariana knew that wasn't strictly true. She loathed the dark and the night, especially since her father died, and now it did not seem quite as dark and the place not quite so lonely.

In fact, there was comfort just knowing that Gian was near.

Finally, whatever it was that had possessed her, that had had her angrily demanding sex, left her.

Oh, Papà!

Gian listened to her cry, and knew that for once it was not for attention. Though it killed him not to go to her, Gian knew they were necessary tears.

He opened the drapes and looked for something to read. Some might call it snooping, but really he was looking for somewhere to charge his phone when a cupboard *fell* open and he could see that this was where *Ariana* had been hiding. It was rather chaotic and piled high with photos, wads and wads of them, and dated boxes too. Ah, so she must have been knee-deep in photos, Gian realised, trying to choose some favourites for the funeral montage. As well as that, there were fashion magazines and blockbusters and recipe books...

An awful lot of them!

Gian selected one and tried to block out her tears by reading. He just stared at the method for tempering white chocolate until finally she fell into silence.

He was reading how to make cannelloni when he heard her again.

It was almost hourly, like some tragic cuckoo clock, but Gian kept the door between them closed for he would *not* sleep with her on the night of her father's funeral. Surely only foolish decisions were made then...

Gian was completely matter-of-fact about sex. To him it was as necessary as breathing. Perhaps it was an exaggeration, but he felt he would not have lived to the age of twenty-five without the escape of it, and he knew he could give her that, but only when her head was clear.

To know she trusted him was significant, for the thought of her misplacing her trust in someone else left him cold.

He watched the black sky turn to a steel grey and, even though Gian knew his logic was flawed, when the silver mist of a new day dawned and he heard her little cry, Gian went through and sat on the bed.

Ariana was far from a temptress at dawn. She covered her face with one hand as he came in, and little bits of last night played like taunting movies.

'Did I make a complete fool of myself?' she asked in a pained voice.

'Of course not,' he said magnanimously, then teased her with a slow smile. 'You just pleaded with me to make love to you.'

'Perhaps it was the cognac,' she said hopefully, but they both knew it had been a small sip and that had been back in Luctano. There had been a lot of walking and talking since then and she could hardly blame the chestnuts! 'I'm sorry for my behaviour. I don't actually fancy you, Gian.'

'Really?'

'Well, sometimes a bit, but then I remind myself that you are just a hunk of good-looking...' She liked his slow smile. 'I remind myself how mean you can be...'

'Mean?'

'*One* glass of champagne at my interview!'

He smiled for he thought she hadn't noticed the absence of a bottle.

'Ah, that.'

'A meal at your bar instead of your restaurant...'

'You make it sound like the local dive.'

'Perhaps, but even so I *deserved* five stars last night. Anyway,' she continued, 'when I do find myself fancying you, I remind myself how remote you can be and how humourless you are.'

'Well, it's good you've come to your senses,' Gian said, 'especially as I don't have condoms with me. I tend not to keep them in my funeral suit.'

She stared back and resisted smiling, determined to prove her humourless point.

'Except we wouldn't need them.' He held up a purple foil packet of contraceptive pills. 'What are these for?'

'You've been snooping.'

'Not really, I wanted toothpaste. I just wondered what you were doing on the Pill if you're not sleeping with anyone...'

'Yet!'

His jaw was set in a grim line. He had this vision of Ariana chasing some bastard who sensed her fragility, yet she was not fragile now. Ariana was looking right at him and there was none of last night's desperate need for comfort, just the desire that had always been beneath it.

'So?' he asked. She looked at the purple Pill packet and was about to lie, as she so often did, and say she was on the Pill for her skin, or so that it made her cycle more predictable, or whatever she would say if her mother found them.

But Gian was certainly not her mother.

And with Gian there was no reason she could see to lie.

'I went on it because I feel like the only person in the world without a sex life, and when I go away with friends I don't want them to know I'm the only one...' She shrugged. 'Pathetic, huh...'

'No more pathetic than when I was younger and would have condoms on me, just to have them on me...'

'Really?'

'Yes.'

They shared a smile in the thin dawn light but then hers wavered. 'Look, I'm sorry I've made things even more awkward between us. I should never have foisted myself on you. I was all a jumble.' She looked at his suave good looks and then at his chest. His tie was gone and his shirt unbuttoned, though just at the top—enough to see a glimpse of chest hair—but she reminded herself of how empty a vessel his chest was and again tried to salvage some pride. 'And it's not as if I enjoyed kissing you last night. In fact, it was like kissing a screen. I felt nothing...'

'Really?'

The thin morning light disappeared as his face came closer, but she refused to be moved by the brush of his lips and the softness of his mouth, just as he had refused to be moved by hers.

Except his kiss was more refined, more

skilled, more measured and she found she could not quite catch her breath as her mouth fought not to relent.

'Like kissing a screen?' he checked.

'Yes,' she said, and felt the scratch of his chin drag on hers. As his fingers came to her jaw, his tongue slipped in, and she absolutely refused to moan at the bliss. In fact, she held her mouth slack as his tongue moved in and out. He tasted divine, all minty and fresh, but there was nothing clean about his kiss—it was filthy, in fact. Thorough, probing and potent with skill, his tongue felt like it ran a wire straight down between her legs and she bunched her hands into fists rather than reach for his head.

'Still nothing?' he checked, and now his hand was stroking her breast through her top and Ariana was sure that if she hadn't been lying down she might have fainted.

'Nothing,' she lied.

'Do you want me to stop?'

'No.'

'Do you understand it is just this once?'

'Oh, stop with the lectures,' she said, as his fingers slid inside her top. 'I accept the terms and conditions...'

He laughed.

Gian actually laughed. Not that she saw it, for he was pulling her T-shirt over her head, and

Ariana was loose limbed and compliant and letting him.

'Please get naked,' she said. 'I want to see you.'

'For a virgin, you certainly know how to provoke me,' Gian commented as he rose from the bed and started to undress.

'Because you provoke me,' Ariana responded. She felt a blush spread across her chest as he removed his shirt and discarded his clothes.

Oh, God. She had always known he was stunning, but he looked so toned, and so male—his chest hair, the thick line on his stomach—and she was holding her breath in nervous, excited anticipation as he unzipped.

He was the most beautiful thing she had seen and she was far from shy, just staring with hungry eyes. It made her blood feel too heavy to move through her heart as he took her hand and closed it around his thick length.

He was warm and hard and he felt like velvet and he let her explore him. Gian kissed her neck, and he kissed down her chest and when his mouth met her breast she wept inside.

'Help me,' she said, because he made her so frantic with desire and his warm hand was on her stomach, which made her want to lift her knees.

'Does that help?' he said, and she moaned as his hand moved down and he stroked her.

'Not enough,' she gasped. 'God, Gian…' And

then she whimpered, for the soft vacuum of his mouth on her breast and the relentless pressure below created a feeling akin to both panic and bliss building inside her.

And though his intention had been to bring Ariana to the edge and then take her, instead he indulged in the pleasure of watching her orgasm build.

Her eyes opened to his for a moment, and she had never felt more bathed in attention, or so in tune with another person.

Then she gave up watching him and shut her eyes, arching her neck as she surrendered to the sumptuous pleasure he so easily gave. He kissed her then so slowly that it felt like a revival but then his thighs were between hers and his mouth was by her temple as her hands held his hips, holding him back, digging him in, both wanting and conflicted. She was desperate for fusion and for the initiation she would allow only Gian to give her.

It hurt, and yet it did not.

He squeezed into her tight space and it was both pleasure and a pain that must surely end. Yet her lungs were expanding and cracks of light returning to the blackout he had brought upon her, and everything multiplied as he moved slowly inside.

'Gian.' She said his name as she had wanted to

since her interview. She rolled it on her tongue and tasted it as he moved deep inside her.

She felt crushed, she felt covered, she felt found. 'Gian,' Ariana said again, as he moved faster, but his name was more like a warning now, for he was tipping her towards the edge and she almost did not want to go.

For then they would end.

'Let go,' he told her. He could feel her slight panic and the mounting tension, and then when she shattered he shot into her in relief.

Both breathless, both dizzy, they lay there, catching their breath.

He adored her inexperience, not just because of the honour of being her first but because she could never know that, even while making love, he held back.

CHAPTER SEVEN

THEY LAY THERE together in silence. Ariana examined her conscience and heart for regret and found none.

Not a jot.

For Gian, there was rare peace as he lay there, their limbs knotted together. Only one thing missing. 'We need food.'

'I have none,' Ariana happily admitted. Her world had been turned upside down since the death of her father, and anyway she tended to eat out. 'Well, I have some ice cream.'

'Ice cream?'

'A lot of ice cream!' Making it was her hobby, her absolute guilty pleasure. Wearing a small wrap, she padded to the kitchen. There she defrosted two croissants and filled them with ice-cream in flavours of cardamom and pistachio and a dark chocolate one too while she waited for the mocha pot to boil and wondered how best to take back her heart.

How to accept his terms and conditions and somehow let him go with grace.

Gian lay there breathing in the scent of brewing coffee, trying to pinpoint the moment he had started wanting her.

On the day of her farcical interview, when he'd first noticed the true colour of her eyes? No, a more honest examination told him it had been before that, and even Ariana herself had voiced it: the night of the silver ball.

Or had it been when she'd swept into the planning meeting and said she wanted silver as a theme?

Instead of gritting his teeth, he had found himself smiling, at least on the inside, for Gian rarely showed how he truly felt.

But, no, while *it* might have started then, for Gian things had really changed the night she had worn silver. Rafael had not been there, and Gian had stood by Ariana's side as she played host. He'd been in awe of how long she'd smiled with the guests and carried on with grace.

He'd wanted to take her aside and tell her that he knew how hard this was, and how proud of her he felt. Instead, they had danced their duty dance and he had held her back from him with rigid arms so she would not feel how turned on he was and how he had ached to drop a kiss on her mouth, on her bare shoulder.

And he was hard for her again.

'Colazione!' Ariana announced breakfast as she came into the room and blinked at his obvious arousal. 'Good grief,' she said. 'I'm far too sore for that.'

'Sore?'

She nodded. 'Nicely sore, the best sore ever.' Oh, God, she wanted him again, but then the ice cream would melt and her phone had already pinged in several messages. She had Nicki coming round *and* she had to do this without starting to cry. 'Eat,' she told him. 'You can have the chocolate one.'

It sounded like she was making a concession, but Gian could tell when she was lying. 'I want the other one.'

'No, no,' she said, 'I'll *let* you have the chocolate one.'

'But I want the pistachio.'

'And cardamom.' Ariana sighed and handed the one she really wanted to him. 'I put in extra when I made it.'

Gian, though used to breakfast in bed, was not used to this—just sitting in bed, eating and tasting food with a woman, and taking bites of each other's.

Bites so big she nearly lost her fingers to his mouth, and they laughed as they fought over food. 'You really made this?' he checked.

'Not the croissant, just the ice cream. I'm going to make salted roast chestnut next, and I shall get them from the same vendor. They were the best I've tasted…'

'They're just chestnuts.'

'No,' she said, and then she gave him the speech she had prepared in her kitchen. 'They kept me warm. *You* kept me warm last night, Gian, even if you did not share my bed. You cared for me last night and then again this morning and I thank you.'

She had surprised him, and then she surprised him further when, with breakfast done, it was Ariana herself who suggested he leave. 'You'd better go. Mamma might drop in.'

'Doesn't she call first?' Gian asked.

'No,' Ariana said. 'I always ask her to but then she reminds me that she's my mother and shouldn't need an appointment…'

'I'll get dressed then.'

'Have a shower,' she offered.

He declined, or he would be trailing a floral boutique all day if he used her scents. 'I'll have one back at the hotel.'

It was odd, Ariana thought as she lay watching him dress, that he did not call La Fiordelise home.

'I like you unshaven,' she admitted. 'You're

always so...' she fought to find the right word '...well-presented and groomed.'

'It's my job to be.'

'Perhaps, but...' She shrugged and his eyes narrowed, trying to interpret yet another of her actions, for those slender shoulders could say many things.

'But what?'

'Nothing.' She smiled wickedly. 'There are other sides to you, I'm sure. I guess I won't find out now.'

'You could. Why not tell the doorman to lie and say you're out?'

'He's so lazy he'd forget,' Ariana rolled her eyes and tried to sound casual, when in truth she wanted to cry and cling onto his leg and beg him to never leave.

Not a good look, that much she knew!

'You really ought to go,' she said as he buckled his belt, though she wanted to reach up and unbuckle it so she was only half listening as he spoke.

'So how do you have a private life, with her dropping in and out? How do you have a...?' And then his voice faded. After all, this morning had been her sex life to date. 'You'll be okay?' he checked as he did up the buttons of his shirt and half tucked it in.

'Yes.'

'If you're not...'

'Gian,' Ariana broke in. 'I have my family and I have my friends.' He hovered on the edge of both of her inner circles but was not fully in either. She felt the indent of the mattress as he sat down and bent over to do up his laces, and though she ached to reach out to him, Ariana told him of the practicalities of her day. 'Also, Nicki is dropping by to tell me about her holiday...'

He sat up and looked right at her. 'As opposed to coming by to see how you're faring after the loss of your father?'

'Of course she's coming for that.' Her eyes narrowed as she took in his sulking mouth; she knew he didn't like Nicki. 'It's a bit early in the relationship for you to be dictating who I see. Oh, that's right, it's not a relationship, and even if it were...' she gave him a tight smile '...that still wouldn't give you a right to say who my friends are, Gian.'

'Fine.' He put up two hands to indicate he was dropping it.

And he was!

Ariana was right. It was not his place to call out her friends but, still, that Nicki got his goat.

All of Ariana's hangers-on did.

'Look,' he said, and Ariana could feel him weighing things up before he spoke. 'I think you were right about working. I do think you'd be an asset for the hotel and if we can both…' He reached over and toyed with a thick coil of her black hair that sat on her collarbone as he spoke, but she pushed his hand away and her response was sudden.

'No!'

She could not work for him; far too much had changed.

'I can't work for you, Gian,' she said, and used another inevitable truth to disguise the real reason. 'Mamma's going to need me now more than ever.'

CHAPTER EIGHT

HER MOTHER DID indeed need her more than ever.

In the tumultuous weeks following her father's death, Ariana's mother's demands were relentless.

It was still by appointment only—Angela Romano liked her make-up, jewellery and the day's carefully chosen wig perfectly arranged before even her daughter dropped around.

Yet the lunches were endless.

As she sat there, twirling a shred of prosciutto on a fork, Ariana fought to quell a surge of anger as her mother called over the sommelier to tell him that the champagne was a little flat. She wondered how someone so supposedly bereft with grief would even notice, let alone have the energy to complain!

'I'm fine, thank you,' Ariana said, placing a hand over her glass. 'I really do need to get going, Mamma,' she said, reaching for her bag. 'I'm meeting Dante.'

'Oh, he can wait.'

'Mamma, please, I said I'd be there at three.' She tried to temper her irritation. 'I really do have to go...' Her voice trailed off because she didn't want to worry her mother, but Dante's mood of late was pretty grim and nothing seemed to be getting done for the Romano Ball—the invitations hadn't even gone out and it was just a few weeks away. 'Would you like me to come over this evening?'

'No, no.' Angela shook her head. 'I have the priest coming over tonight.'

'Well, take care.' Ariana kissed her on both cheeks. 'I shall see you soon.'

'Tomorrow,' Angela checked. 'Here? Or perhaps we could go shopping...' She ran a disapproving eye over Ariana's navy shift dress and espadrilles. 'We could get you something a little less last year.'

Ariana had never felt more stifled and wished not for the first time that there was more purpose and structure to her day. She took a taxi to Romano Holdings in the EUR district, craning her neck as they passed La Fiordelise. She wished she was working there.

And then she flushed with sheer pleasure when she recalled the very reason she now could not.

It was her favourite memory, a harbour in troubled times she could return to, yet there was confusion there too—how, from the very moment they had kissed, Gian had started the countdown to the end.

She had stopped having drinks there on a Friday. Well, Paulo had been banned and Nicki said they should no longer go in solidarity with their friend.

Except Ariana had loved going there…

'Signorina?'

The voice of the driver startled her and Ariana realised they had arrived. Time tended to run away whenever she thought of Gian, and so she determinedly put him out of her mind as she walked into the plush office building.

Sarah, Dante's PA, gave her a smile. 'Go through,' she said and then added, 'Good luck.'

'Do I need it?' Ariana joked, but then all joking faded when she saw him. 'Dante!' She could not keep the surprise from her voice when she saw her older brother, looking less than his put-together self, for his complexion was grey and his shirt was crumpled and there was just such a heavy air to him. 'How are you doing?' she asked as she went over and kissed his cheeks and gave him a hug. 'I've barely seen you. Mamma is saying the same.'

'Well, work has been busy.'

'I'm sure it has.' She nodded. 'What's happening about the ball?'

'It's all under control. I'm meeting with Gian at five to finalise the details…' His voice trailed off. There was a strange atmosphere in the office, and for an appalling moment she wondered if Dante had found out about their one illicit night, or rather illicit morning.

'And?' she asked with a nervous laugh. 'What are the final details?'

Dante said nothing.

'How are we addressing Papà's passing?' Ariana pushed.

'I'm sure Gian will take care of that.'

'But in the will Papà asked that his children take care of the ball,' Ariana said, but then stopped and sat chewing the edge of her thumbnail. She was worried about Dante. Though not as close to him as she had always been to Stefano, she knew there was something wrong. He was grieving for their father, but she couldn't help but think there was more to it than that. 'Is everything okay, Dante?' she ventured.

'Of course.'

'You can talk to me. I might just understand.' He closed his eyes, as if she couldn't possibly. 'Look, why don't I meet with Gian?' There was genuinely no ulterior motive, just a need to get the ball right for their father. 'I can take over the ball…'

'Would you?' Dante's relief was evident.

'Of course.' Ariana nodded.

It was only then that her nerves caught up!

Ariana walked by the *laghetto* for a full hour. The cherry blossoms were in full bloom and the park looked stunning, and if there was a little trepidation about coming face to face with Gian it was soon displaced as something else took hold. Excitement. It felt like for ever since her brain had been put to work.

Sitting on a bench, looking at the blossom swirl and float like pink snow, it was the perfect place for her imagination to wander. Scrabbling in her bag, she took out a journal and started to make notes.

It was exhilarating, cathartic, and there were tears in her eyes as memories danced while words formed on the page. It was right that she take over the ball, Ariana knew, for she knew how best to celebrate her father.

Ariana wasn't even nervous about facing Gian.

She had so much to tell him.

'I have Ariana Romano in Reception to see you,' Luna informed him.

'Ariana?' Gian frowned. 'But I thought I was meeting with Dante…'

'Well, Ariana is here instead.'

'Fine.' Gian did his level best to act as if it

were of no consequence that it was Ariana who had just arrived. It was an informal meeting, but also a very *necessary* meeting. One that Gian had pushed for, given Dante seemed to have—both figuratively and literally—dropped the ball. 'Send her through.'

Damn.

Gian usually had no qualms about facing an ex-lover, but with Ariana it felt different indeed.

It was because they were family friends, he told himself, steadfastly refusing to examine his feelings further than that.

It had been weeks since the funeral and to his quiet surprise he had heard nothing from Ariana. He had expected the demanding, rather clingy Ariana to drape herself like bindweed around one of the columns in Reception, or at the very least find an *accidental* reason for her to drop by.

And now she was here.

He was curious as to her mood, and very determined to get things back on a more regular footing, as if they had never made love.

As if they had not sat eating ice cream naked in her bed.

She stepped into his office, and brought with her an Italian spring. He had to consciously remind himself to greet her the same way he would have before…

'Ariana…' He stood and went round his desk

and of course kissed her cheeks. There were dots of pink blossom in her hair and he had to resist lifting his hand and carefully picking them out. 'This is unexpected…'

'I know.' She gave him an apologetic smile and an eye-roll as she took her seat but she was too excited to be awkward around him. 'Dante and I agreed that I will take over the final preparations for the ball. Believe me, I did not engineer it…'

He knew she spoke the truth.

For Ariana with a secret agenda would be immaculate, rather than bare-legged and a little tousled. Plus, she was more animated than he had ever seen her and dived straight in.

'Firstly, I don't want to go with the forest theme…'

'Thank God,' Gian said. 'What theme do you have in mind?'

'None,' Ariana said. 'I want the ballroom to speak for itself, and I want gardenias on each table. He loved them.'

'Yes.'

'And orchids…' she said, but Gian reacted with a wavering gesture with his hand.

'Not together,' he said.

'Perhaps by his photo?'

Gian nodded.

'And I want to change the menu.' She handed him a sheet of paper she had torn from a pad.

He said nothing as he read through it, for Ariana did all the talking. 'These were my father's favourites,' she said. 'I thought we could use some produce from his estate…'

'One moment,' Gian said. She sat tapping her feet as, suddenly in the midst of this most important meeting, he simply got up and walked out. 'Sorry about that,' he said a moment later when he returned. 'Now, where were we?'

'I don't think it should be a solemn night, but if we can acknowledge him in the food and wine…'

She spoke for almost two hours. There was no champagne brought in, just sparkling water, which she took grateful sips of between pouring out ideas. There was no flirting, no reference to what had happened, no alluding to it, just a determination to get this important night right.

'What about the wording for the invitations?' Gian said. 'Mia is technically the host…'

'No!' Only then did she flare. 'We don't even know if she's coming.'

'I'll work on the wording,' Gian agreed. 'Leave Mia to me. I think your ideas are excellent. There's a lot to do but I agree it has to be perfect. Why don't we try the dinner menu now?'

'Now?' she frowned.

'I asked Luna to give your menu to my head chef. He is preparing a sample menu…'

She had her dinner invitation.

He never took dates to the hotel's restaurant, but Ariana wasn't his date. It was business, Gian told himself as they were shown to his table. It looked out onto the restaurant but was private enough for conversation to take place.

'I wish I was better dressed,' Ariana admitted as a huge napkin was placed in her lap. Her clothes were better suited for lunch, or even a gentle lakeside walk, certainly not fine dining in La Fiordelise.

'You look…' He hesitated, for he did not tell his business dates they looked stunning or beautiful. 'Completely fine.' Gian settled for that, yet it felt as flat as the iced water that was being poured, and as shallow as the bowl in which a waterlily floated. 'You look stunning,' Gian admitted. 'Especially with pink blossom in your hair.'

Ariana laughed and raked a hand through her mane. 'I was walking by the office; the blossom is out and it's so beautiful.'

'And so fleeting.'

Like us, she wanted to say as she dropped a few petals from her hair into the water lily bowl between them. 'Yes, so fleeting,' Ariana agreed, 'but worth it.'

It was the briefest, and the only reference to what they had shared.

The starter was ravioli stuffed with pecorino with a creamy white truffle sauce and it brought a smile to her lips as it was placed on the table and she signalled the waiter to rain pepper upon it.

'Taste it first,' he told her.

'Why?' she said. 'If it is cooked to my father's taste then to my mind it needs more pepper and a little less salt.' She signalled to the waiter for even more.

'You love your pepper.'

'I do! And he loved this pasta so much.'

'I know,' Gian told her. 'It was served on the night La Fiordelise came back to life.' He put down his fork and though he had never told another living soul the details, if ever there was a time to, it was now. 'Your father saved La Fiordelise.'

'Saved it?'

'Yes. It was practically empty of guests and running on a skeleton staff when my family died.'

She looked up.

'Papà gave you a loan?'

'Not as such.'

Ariana frowned.

'I inherited a disaster,' Gian said, 'and, believe me, the banks agreed...' He hesitated at how much to tell her and decided, for this part of

Rafael's life at least, there was no need for brevity and so as the main course was served he told her what had happened. 'Your father suggested buying into the business.'

'Really?' Ariana hadn't known that. 'But he didn't?'

'No.' Gian shook his head. 'I refused his offer.'

'Can I ask why?'

'I prefer to rise or fall alone,' Gian said. 'I did not see that the hotel could be saved. Still, not everyone was aware that it was on the brink of going under, and I told your father about a request to host some royalty on their trip to Rome. Top secret, of course...

'I couldn't consider it, but your father said it was a chance to turn things around. The Penthouse Suite was still incredible—my parents always kept the best for themselves—and the dining room was, of course, in good shape. And so word got around...'

'How?' Ariana frowned. 'If it was top secret?'

Gian smiled. 'He told your mother.' There was a tiny feeling of triumph to see Ariana laugh. 'Before we knew it, the hotel was at full quota for a certain weekend in February.'

'Really?'

'The helicopter brought in the best produce from your father's estate and the best wines. And my staff worked like they never had before. That's why now I only hire staff who can work in all areas. I had the chief bartender making up suites. Luna herself got the Penthouse Suite ready...'

'My goodness.'

'It was the biggest charade and it went off superbly and La Fiordelise shuddered back to life.'

'Just like that?'

'Not just like that,' Gian corrected. 'Years of hard work.'

The main course was just as delicious but when it came to dessert, Ariana could not choose from her father's favourites, which were all being served.

'I think we choose the two best, and of course ice cream,' Gian said, 'though not this.' He frowned as his silver spoon sliced through a quenelle of ice cream from her menu and pulled a face as he tasted it. 'Tutti-frutti?'

'It was his favourite,' Ariana said. 'Every summer, in the evening, he would send me to the shop to get a cone for him.'

'Really?' Gian checked, and he watched a little flush of pink spread up her neck. 'Because I seem to remember that you would go to the store for ice cream and when you came back with this flavour your *papà* always declined his cone.'

'No.' She shook her head. 'You have it wrong.'

'And Stefano would complain that he didn't

like tutti-frutti either, and so you would end up having to eat all three.'

'You're getting mixed up,' Ariana said haughtily, and she dipped her spoon into the quenelle. He watched as she took a taste and closed her eyes in bliss, then opened them to him and looked right at him. 'He *loved* that ice cream.'

Rafael probably had, Gian conceded. Not so much the sickly-sweet candied ice cream, more the little games Ariana constantly played.

'Well, it's not going on the menu,' Gian said. 'It's…' He dismissed it with a wave of his hand. 'A simple *affogato* is a better way to round off the meal.' He watched her pout. 'Ariana, you are one of the few people in the world who like tutti-frutti ice cream. Trust me on that.'

'I suppose you know best,' she said in her best pained voice.

'There is no suppose about it.'

'It would mean so much to me, though…'

Wearily he took another taste and, as he did so, Ariana did her sneaky best and pulled on all her inner resources so that crocodile tears pooled in her violet eyes.

It did nothing to move that black heart, though.

'No,' Gian said, and put down his spoon and, as if to prove how awful her dessert of choice was, took a drink of water before speaking again.

'Would you like some *amaro* or a cognac?' Gian suggested, but Ariana shook her head.

'No, thank you.'

'Are you sulking?' he asked.

'A little bit,' she admitted, and then smiled despite herself. 'Of course not. I just ought to get home…' She looked away then, because the reason she could not stay was surely there in her eyes.

She wanted her cognac.

But not here.

Ariana wanted to curl up with him elsewhere, to talk, to kiss, but most dangerous of all she actually ached to know him better.

And if she stayed she would cross a line. The business meeting had surely concluded and to keep it at that, she needed to leave. 'Thank you for a lovely dinner.'

'I'll arrange a car—'

'Gian,' she cut in, 'the concierge can do that.'

'Then I'll walk you out.'

They stood at the entrance and tried to pretend that they had never tumbled naked into bed, had never been more than old friends.

'Your ideas are excellent,' Gian said as the doorman blew his whistle to summon a vehicle.

'Except for dessert.'

'Except for dessert,' he agreed.

'And you think it's okay not to have a theme?'

'I think it's better.' Gian nodded. 'It's going to be a tricky night…'

'Yes,' Ariana agreed.

They had been over this already. The car pulled up and it was time to stay or leave.

'Gian—' she started, for she wanted so badly to ask why there was no possible hope for them.

'I'll say goodnight,' Gian cut in, because if he didn't he would break his own rules about separate lives and kiss her beneath the lights and take her to his private apartment where no lover had ever gone. And they would take things further than he'd ever dared, for no one was permitted a place in his closed-off heart.

And so he kissed her on both cheeks, and as he did so a little pink petal that had been hanging temptingly from a strand of her jet-black hair, just waiting for him to pick it off, glided down to his lapel. Her eyes drifted down. 'You're wearing my blossom.'

He glanced down. 'Yes.'

She would not be Svetlana, Ariana decided, and pick it off. Or one of the doubtless many others that had come before her and dared to demand more. She bunched her fist so hard that her nails dug into her palm, and smiled. 'You'd better tidy yourself up then.'

To her everlasting credit, Ariana got into the car and went home alone.

CHAPTER NINE

BY AND BY, the Romano Ball drew closer.

Gian had quickly forged a strictly business code.

There were emails and phone calls and even a couple of face-to-face meetings, but there was no low-level flirting or alluding to *them*.

For there was no them.

If anything, it was all so professional that Ariana actually wondered if she'd completely misread the mood that night after dinner, if it really had all been just business to him.

Sometimes she wondered what might have happened if she hadn't asked him to leave her apartment that morning, because she'd been unable to grasp at the time that it really was to be the end of them.

Sometimes she just stared into space for a whole afternoon, blinking as she realised it was getting dark, just wondering about him.

A man who did not want love.

Everyone breathed a private sigh of relief when

Angela Romano, unable to bear Rome at the time of the Romano Ball, headed off on a cruise.

Phew!

Ariana lay in bed, so relieved not to have to do lunch and placate her mother as well as focus her attention on both Stefano and Eloa's wedding, which she was now helping with a little, and organise the ball.

Even when the final menu cards came, Ariana merely fired back a confirmation, saying that they looked wonderful and she was certain her father would approve.

There was not as much as a breath of tutti-frutti between them.

Or references to pink blossom.

Or hints about a moonlit night and a deep kiss by the eternal flame.

It was just:

Gian, regarding the orchids, Roberto will bring them on the day...

Blah, blah, blah...

And in turn Gian, kept to his side of the deal. Or he tried to.

Ariana, regarding the seating plan...

But two days from the big day, he was finally so irritated that he picked up the phone and called her. 'I don't understand the problem with Nicki,' Gian said. 'We managed to find her a seat…' He chose not to add that Nicki was being accommodated at the exclusion of a potential paying guest and this ball was a very high-end ticket indeed. 'What is her issue?'

'The table is near the back,' Ariana explained, 'and with Paulo not coming because you banned him—'

'I will ban anyone who is abusive to my staff, which he was.'

'Well, she doesn't know anyone she's seated with. She was hoping to bring a friend.'

'*You're* her friend,' Gian rather tersely pointed out. 'Would you like me to move you to sit with her, because there simply isn't room at the top table.'

'Don't be ridiculous,' Ariana said. 'Has Mia RSVP'd yet?'

He knew, even before she asked, that Nicki must have asked her the same question 'Because, if she doesn't come then there'll be a space.'

'Ariana.' It was the first time they had crossed to anything remotely personal. 'I told both you and Dante that you are to leave Mia to me.'

'Yes, but if she isn't even coming…'

'You cannot give Mia's place to…' *to one of your freeloaders*, he was tempted to add, but refrained and reminded himself that this was a business discussion. In truth, if the Romanos wanted a flock of geese seated at the head table then it was his job to accommodate it. He took a breath. Where Ariana was concerned, it was almost impossible to draw the line and differentiate between personal and professional. 'However,' Gian said, 'if you want Nicki at the top table so desperately then she can have my seat.'

'But where would you sit?' Ariana asked, loathing the thought of him not being next to her. Gian was always seated by her side at the Romano Ball, but now it seemed like he was willing to break that tradition.

'In the seat to which she is currently assigned. I'll be working the room anyway. Nicki can have my seat, if that is what you want.'

'No, no,' Ariana rapidly broke in, blushing as she declined his cold and practical solution to salvage her seat beside Gian. 'Just leave it as it is.'

'Very well,' Gian clipped. 'Anything else?'

'I don't think so. Should there be?'

'No.' Gian was assured. 'Everything is under control.'

Except himself, but he was working on that, determined to erase that forbidden morning from his thoughts.

He did not need the complication of Ariana Romano in his life, he insisted to himself. He just had to get past the ball.

It wasn't just Ariana that was worrying him, though.

Trouble loomed in another Romano direction…

'Dante!' Gian shook his friend's hand and invited him to take a seat when he arrived unannounced the day before the ball. 'I just spoke with Ariana this morning…'

'I hear it's all under control.'

'She's done very well,' Gian agreed. 'I expect the ball to be a huge success. Your sister has an eye for detail—'

'Has Mia responded?' Dante cut in.

'Not as yet,' Gian said. 'As I said to Ariana, even if she arrives unannounced, she will be greeted as if she had always been expected and made to feel most welcome.'

'Well, if that's the case, could you ensure she gets this gift just before she heads down to the ball?' He handed Gian a black velvet box and envelope. 'I thought it better to take care of the hostess gift myself, rather than leave it to Ariana.' He gave a black laugh. 'Or it would be a doll full of pins…'

Dante was his close friend, yet Gian found himself smiling his on-duty smile. 'Of course. I'll see to it personally.'

'And perhaps it would be best not to upset Ariana with such details…'

'Naturalmente,' Gian said.

Damn, he thought.

By and by, the Romano Ball loomed ever closer.

Gian wanted the ball over and done with; he wanted Ariana gone, instead of her voice, her emails, her thoughts all dancing in his mind.

He wanted his life back to neat order, with sex when he required it and no silent demands for a future.

Gian could feel how much she wanted him, which was usually a turn-off.

He found, though, that he liked it that she craved him and yet kept herself under control. He did his best to ignore it as another damned message pinged into his box, with an attachment.

And there, smiling at him, was his friend Rafael.

It was a slight shock.

Unexpected.

He stared back at Rafael and silently swore that he would stay the hell away from hurting his daughter.

Ariana. Yes, the photo you found of Rafael on Ponte Vecchio was most suitable. Kind regards, Gian

Ariana scoured in between the lines for even the slightest sign, the tiniest clue, that he might linger there in the memory of them, but there was not a single needle she could glean in the haystack.

There were no veiled clues or promises.

His briefly open heart had, it would seem, ever so politely, closed.

By and by, a silver car pulled up outside La Fiordelise in the late afternoon on the day of the Romano Foundation Ball.

And trouble loomed large.

'Ariana Romano is here,' Luna informed him. 'You wanted to see her when she arrived.'

'Yes.'

'Shall I send her through?'

'Of course.'

'Gian!'

She smiled her red-lipped smile and for someone running later than the Mad Hatter, she still looked pretty incredible in a loose top that showed one shoulder and a skirt that showed a lot of leg.

Gian, though, did not look his usual self.

'You look…' she started, but then stopped. It was none of her business that the immaculate Gian was unshaven and that his tie was pulled loose. No doubt he was saving his shave for the evening, but the unrufflable Gian looked, well, ruffled.

She wanted to hold him, to climb onto his knee

and kiss that tense face, but instead she stood stock still.

'Ariana…' He got up and they did the kiss-kiss thing.

'Careful,' she warned, so he didn't crush the orchids. 'Damn things,' she added as he re-took his seat but Ariana did not sit down. 'Who knew flowers could cause so much trouble. Roberto is sick and can't come,' Ariana explained, nerves making her mouth run away. 'And these were the orchids he was supposed to bring…' She held up her free hand in an exasperated gesture. 'I've been standing on a platform at Roma Termini, waiting for a courier to deliver them.'

'It's fine.' He tried not to want her; he tried to treat her as he once would have. 'Do you want a drink?'

'I don't have time for a drink,' Ariana pointed out. 'I have to be greeting guests in a couple of hours. What did you want to see me about?'

He was silent for a moment as he poured his own drink while wondering how best to broach things. 'Mia is here.'

'So?' Ariana shrugged and turned to go. 'What do I care? There was no need to drag me to your office. You could have told me that in a text.'

'Yes.' He watched the tension in her jaw and the press of her lips and knew she was struggling to process the news. Aside from that, there was also a whole lot more she didn't know.

Dante and Mia had the adjoining presidential suites.

And Dante had the key.

Yes, Gian De Luca was the keeper of many secrets and at times it was hell. 'I want to speak to you,' he said. 'About tonight.'

'You're going to tell me to behave and be nice. Don't worry. I've already had the lecture from Dante. Poor Mia is struggling to face us all tonight. Poor Mia—'

'Ariana!' He spoke more harshly then, but that was like holding up a red rag to a bull, Gian knew, for nothing tamed her. 'Do you remember how you felt at your father's funeral, as if everything might get out of hand? Well, Mia is surely feeling that way...'

'*Poor* Mia, you mean.' She looked at him then, really looked, and she could see the fan of lines beside his eyes and feel his tension. She assumed he was concerned about Mia; it never entered her head that his concern might be for her. 'Why do you always take her side?' Ariana asked, jealousy rearing its ugly head. 'Don't tell me you have a thing for her too...' She simply could not bear it if that was the case, and spite got the better of her. 'Well, I guess at least she's closer to your age than Papà's.'

'Enough!' Gian cut in. 'Why do you have to be so petty and cruel whenever you speak about her?'

'Because I hate her.' Ariana shrugged. 'And I hate it that my parents divorced. I'll never forgive her.'

'You forgave your father when it was he who had the affair. Mia, at the time, was single.'

'Stop it,' Ariana said, loathing his logic. 'And please stop telling me what to think and how to feel. We slept with each other once—that doesn't give you licence to police my friends and now how I interact with my family.'

'You're insufferable, Ariana.' He strode over and took her bare arms. He wanted to shake some sense into her, but even as he scolded her Gian actually understood her anger more than she knew.

Ariana was only ever given half-truths.

Or a quarter.

Or an eighth.

The Romanos were masters at smoke and mirrors and Ariana had grown up stumbling blind through their labyrinth of lies, and he loathed it that he was only giving her a tiny sliver of the truth now.

'I'm trying…' He held on to his words, because if he said one thing more it might well be too much. 'I'm trying to ensure that this night goes well.'

'Have you delivered Mia this pre-function lecture?' Ariana goaded. 'Have Stefano and Dante been summoned too? No!' She answered for him. 'Because you don't trust me.'

'No, because I—' Gian abruptly halted himself, because he didn't want to admit, even to himself, that he cared about Ariana more than he wanted to. 'Because I know how you feel about Mia, and I also know that you want the night to be a success.'

'Then we want the same thing,' Ariana replied tartly.

They did indeed want the same thing and now they were face to face in no way that could be construed as professional.

She looked up at him through narrowed eyes. She wanted to exit in a huff, but his hands were on her bare arms and she liked the odd comfort of him, of someone, the first person ever, pulling her back before she went too far.

They were both breathing hard, as if they had just kissed.

Ariana looked at his mouth and unshaven jaw and felt his fingers holding the top of her arms. He turned her on so easily that she could feel the heat at the top of her legs, and the ache of her breasts in her flimsy bra. She knew he was hard, she just knew, the same way she did not need to look at the sky to know it was darkening.

'Ariana,' Gian said in a voice that sounded a touch gravelly, 'if there are any issues tonight, then you are to come to me.'

She always did, Ariana realised.

Whether it was stolen chocolate, or her father's widow showing up, she always leaned on Gian, yet she could not when it came to the urgent matter of her heart, for he was the one who was quietly stealing it.

'I need to get on,' Ariana croaked.

'Of course,' Gian politely agreed.

'And you need to shave.'

When she had gone, Gian opened up the safe and took out the black box and envelope.

He would not break his own rules and deliberately did not look inside.

He would go and get ready and then drop off the gift to Mia, and then get through this night and once that was done, hopefully he wouldn't have to see Ariana for some considerable time.

Except that was easier said than done. First he had to dance with her and hold her and for the first time ever he found he wanted someone in his life.

And so he reminded himself of all the reasons why he did not want someone in his life.

When he should have been meeting with the

barber in his apartment and then seeing to the final preparations for this important night, instead he took out the official papers he did his level best to avoid.

It was all there.

The drugs, the debauchery, the *findings*… The absolute hell of love.

For he had loved them.

Even if his parents had not wanted him.

And he had loved his brother Eduardo, even if it had been safer to stop caring, to detach and close off his heart.

To refuse all drama.

And Ariana really was pure drama.

'Gian?' Luna knocked on his door a long time later and found him sitting almost in the dark. 'Should you still be here?'

'No,' he admitted, and stood. 'Luna,' he said, 'can you…?' He was about to hand over the papers to shred. 'It doesn't matter,' Gian said, and returned them to the safe in case he ever needed another reminder of why he refused to let someone into his life.

And, by and by, the Romano Foundation Ball was here.

CHAPTER TEN

ARIANA WORE BLACK.

A simple black velvet halter neck and the diamond studs her parents had given her for her eighteenth.

She put on her red lips, though, and lashings of mascara. There was a ridiculous pit of anticipation building at the thought of dancing with Gian, for she was still floating from the encounter in his office and getting her hopes up as she made her way down for the ball.

His warning, however poorly she'd taken it, meant that Ariana was at least slightly prepared when her father's *widow* made her entrance. And what an entrance. Mia was standing at the top of the stairs in crimson! Her blonde hair was piled up, and heavy diamond earrings glittered at her ears as she made her way down. Ariana saw red—as red as the dress that Mia wore.

'So much for the grieving widow,' she hissed to Dante.

She was, in fact, grateful to Gian for the heads-up and even managed a somewhat stilted greeting to the widow in red, but then all rancour drained from her when she saw Gian approach.

He was still unshaven, but sexily so.

His attire was immaculate and his black hair gleaming but it was such a change from his more regular suave appearance at such an event that she felt a pull, down low. He simply hollowed her out with desire.

'Eloa,' he said in that low, throaty drawl. Even the happily engaged, blissfully-in-love Eloa had the hormones to blush when bathed in his attention. 'You look exquisite.' He kissed her cheeks and then shook Stefano's hand. 'Dante.' He nodded to his friend. 'I trust everything is satisfactory.'

'Absolutely.' Dante agreed.

He turned to Ariana, finally acknowledging her. Sort of. His eyes did not as much as dust over her body, and she felt the chill of a snub, even as he spoke politely. 'Ariana, you look beautiful.'

They were the same words he said every year when he greeted her at the ball, and he kissed her on the cheeks as he always did when they met, except he barely whispered past her skin.

As if she were an old aunt, Ariana thought.

'Thank you,' she said. 'Everything looks beautiful.' And then she leaned in and murmured, 'Even the grieving widow.'

He didn't smile, and neither did he return her little in joke.

There was an edge to him that she couldn't quite define, an off-limits sign she could almost read. He was essentially ignoring her.

Damn you, Gian, she thought as she headed into the ballroom. But really she was cross with herself. Somewhere, somehow, she had lost sight of the clear message he had given right at the start and had been foolish enough to get her hopes up.

The ballroom could never be described as understated, but without hanging moons and ivy vines tonight it looked its elegant best, and Ariana caught the sweet scent of gardenias as she took her seat. Mia entered and took her seat at the table too, Gian sitting between them. He was, of course, his usual dignified self and made polite small talk alternately with both Mia and Ariana.

Like a parent wedged between two warring siblings and trying to give both equal attention, Ariana thought.

'I shouldn't have worn red,' Mia said as the pasta was served. 'It was the gown I had for last year...'

'You look stunning,' Gian told her—*again*. And Ariana gritted her teeth.

Gian tried his level best to be his usual self, as Ariana smouldered beside him. The drama of waiting for her to explode was painful, but he told himself she was not his problem. He told himself that the Romanos, the whole lot of them, were each a theatre production in themselves.

The bed-hopping, the scandals—Dante and Mia doing their best not to make eye contact. He was rather certain that the heavy earrings she wore had been in the box that he had earlier delivered to her door. Rafael's lover was too ill to attend but his orchids took pride of place. Eloa and Stefano were desperate for the night to be over so they could be alone.

And don't get me started on Ariana, he thought.

He could feel her, smell her, hear her when she spoke, and of course she was asking for more pepper.

She jangled his nerves and she beguiled him, because for once she behaved.

Almost.

She turned her back when Mia tried to speak, which he did his level best to ignore and gloss over.

And then the appalling Nicki came over between courses and moaned about her seat. 'Ariana, you really have stuck me beside the most boring people and I'll never hear the speeches back there.'

Gian stared ahead, but said in a low voice for Ariana's ears, 'My offer still stands.'

He would move, Ariana knew. Right now, Gian would get up and stalk off and it was the last thing she wanted. She looked at her friend and, for the first time ever, stood up for herself. 'Nicki, the sound engineer is the best in Rome. I'm sure you'll be able to hear.'

Well done, he wanted to tell her. *Well done, Ariana.*

But he stayed silent. It was not his place.

Yet he wanted it to be.

There was just one unkind comment, as dessert was being served, when Eloa spoke of her wedding that was now just a few short weeks away. She told Mia, 'Ariana is helping us organise a few things,' clearly trying to feed her into the conversation.

'Yes.' Ariana flashed a red-lipped smile at Mia. 'It's going to be amazing. Anyone who's anyone has been invited…'

Meaning—*not you!*

Gian caved.

Ariana felt his hand on her thigh, and the grip of his fingers actually halted her words.

'That's not a good idea,' she said to Gian, while looking ahead. 'If you reward me each time I go too far…'

'Would you prefer the discipline method?'

She threw her head back and laughed.

Even with Mia at her table, Ariana found that with Gian beside her she could still have such a wonderful night.

And it was then that she got another reward, for as the desserts were served and shots of coffee were tossed over ice creams, there was a special dish, made just for her. Tutti-frutti.

Ariana gasped.

'Yes.'

It was better than being handed chestnuts on a freezing night; it was better than a sliver of gold when she could not face her father's funeral alone.

'Thank you.'

She wanted to cry as she tasted the sweet candied ice cream and remembered how her father had, over and over, let her get away with buying three cones, just so she could devour them all.

Happy memories reigned as little shots of sugar burst on her tongue and when she finished she had to dab at her eyes with her napkin. 'Ice cream has never made me cry before,' she admitted to Gian as the waiter cleared her very clean plate. 'Happy tears, though. It was beautiful, thank you.'

'Shall we get it over with?' Gian asked as the band struck up.

'Get what over with?' Ariana said, as if she didn't know.

'The duty dance.'

It had been months since she had known the bliss of his arms, and for Gian it had been months with no feminine pleasure.

He'd known he would only be thinking of her and, besides, no one else had her scent.

'Your perfume,' he said, as he held her at a distance and resumed their old wars.

'I've told you,' she said, 'I don't wear any.' She looked right at him. 'You're the only one who complains.'

'I'm not complaining.'

'Why do you always hold me at such a distance?'

'You know why,' he said, and pulled her deep in so she could feel him hard against the softness of her stomach. She flared to the scent of citrus and bergamot and testosterone and the roughness of his skin seemed to burn her rouged cheek. 'You didn't shave…'

'Because you like me unshaven.'

'Gian.' She was trying to breathe and dance and deal with the change all at the same time. She simply didn't understand him. 'You've ignored me most of the night…'

'I tried to,' he admitted.

'You've ignored me for weeks…' He shook

his head, but then nodded when she quoted his impersonal sign-offs. *'"Kind regards, Gian"?'*

'How else could we get the ball done?'

'And after tonight will you ignore me again?'

He didn't answer because he didn't know. He could not afford to think of tomorrow now.

The judgements of the coroner's report should be flicking through his mind, except tonight those violet eyes turned his warning systems off.

He gave her no promises, just told her the card for his private elevator would be in her bag and left her to stumble her way through the rest of the evening.

The speeches were brilliant, the whole night was perfect, but it felt as though she might faint with desire as she said farewell to the guests.

'We should go for a drink in the bar,' Nicki said.

'It will be closed.'

'I meant the bar in your room.' Nicki smiled, but Ariana shook her head. 'I'm exhausted, Nicki.'

It was a lie.

Ariana felt as alive as an exposed wire as she slipped away and took the private elevator to his floor and let herself in.

It was not the view that she craved, or the stunning surroundings; it was the glimpses of him.

There were paintings, the sketches of Fiordelise he had told her about, his history and lineage all there on the walls.

The older Dukes and Duchesses too, and it went right down to his parents, his brother...

But where was Gian?

Her eyes scanned the walls.

Where was the man she adored?

Then she found him, in a suit, at the desk in Reception, and she frowned at the one single image of him, but her thoughts faded as she heard the whir of the elevator. And her heart moved to her throat as he stepped through the door.

It had been agony not to touch him, but both were relieved of that agony now.

As they reached for each other, almost ran to each other, it was like falling into another dimension.

He was undoing her gown so it fell like a black puddle on the floor. His tongue was cool and his kisses hot as she impatiently pushed down the sleeves of his jacket, and they were so *desperate* for each other, for more than this.

He picked her up, dressed only in her underwear, and deposited her onto a vast gold bed.

His eyes never left her face as Ariana removed her bra and lay on her back, propped up by her elbows and watching him undress.

He threw off the tie as though it was choking

him and she gave a satisfied smile when the cufflinks dropped silently to the carpet for he was as desperate as she.

He slowed down to take off her strappy high heels. First the right, and he was so annoyingly slow with the strap that she took her other high heel and pressed it into his toned stomach.

Gian caught her calf.

She could see his erection, the one that had been pressed against her on the dance floor, and she almost writhed in frustration as he took off her left high heel. Now the soles of her feet were on his stomach as he slowly pulled her silk knickers down, revealing her to him. Finally, he buried his face in her.

'Gian!' She was shocked at the delicious roughness of him, at the sounds of him, at her own reaction to him, for she was coming as quickly as that.

Suddenly she was pulsing as he devoured her and then she was falling where she lay, but with him atop her.

'We need condoms…' she said frantically, for she had cursed herself after the last time.

'There's been no one since.'

Those words made her too weak for reason.

He was holding her naked as she tumbled through space, and for all the terrible decisions she had made in her lifetime, this, Ariana knew, was not one of them.

He kissed her mouth and her face, the shells of her ears, and the tender skin of her neck as he took her.

He devoured her and rained kisses and words on her that should not be said to someone you were not prepared to love the next day.

'You make me crazy,' he told her.

And that made her heart sing.

He told her how he had wanted her all night, how he had wanted her for weeks, in fact, all this as he moved within her and stared right into her eyes. The prolonged intensity astounded her, the focus, the climb, the ache of want and the desire to give. Her hips moved involuntarily with his and they were wild for each other, rolling and tumbling across the bed. He took in her flushed features and brushed the damp hair back from her face as he drove into her and gazed at her.

Help, Ariana thought, for she had never seen Gian so tender before.

There was passion and there was desire, but there was something else too.

He was also aware of it, this slip into a deeper caring, this moment, when he rolled her onto her back again, and one lesson in tenderness moved to the next.

He was up on his forearms, his body sliding

over hers, each intimate stroke of him winding her tighter and tighter. His pace built and built and she wrapped her legs around his hips and simply clung on as he took her to wherever he chose.

He took her to bliss, pounding her senses, making her more his with each thrust.

For Gian it was a dangerous space. He knew that as he looked down at her, her black hair splayed on his pillow, her body tight around his. He would regret this later, Gian knew, but at that moment he didn't care.

Especially as he swelled that delicious final time and filled her. Completely.

And this time it was Gian shouting out her name.

He dragged her into an orgasm so deep and intense that for a moment she existed there with him.

It was dizzying...too much...never enough, and she was crying as it was fading.

And he kissed her back to consciousness.

'I loved my ice cream,' she told him, and then stopped, because there was another thing that Ariana knew she loved too.

Don't say it, she told herself as he turned off the lights with a single bedside switch and Ariana curled into him, loving the feel of being utterly spent yet curiously awake in her lover's arms.

Ariana usually hated the dark and the night, but not this night. The thud-thud-thud of his heart and the sound of Gian collecting his breath brought Ariana a sense of contentment in the soft thrum of her body as she came down from the high he had taken her to.

'Why are there no paintings or sketches of Violetta?'

'There are a couple but they need to be restored.'

'And why are there no photos of you?' Ariana asked a question that could only be asked in the dark, in that black hole where gravity did not apply, where words floated and drifted in nonsensical patterns, before logic applied.

'There are,' he said. 'There's one in the gallery, taken during the royal visit to La Fiordelise—in the entrance hall.'

'You mean the Employee of the Month photo?' Ariana said, mocking his formal business photo. For some reason her words made them both laugh.

But then the laughter faded.

'Why are there no photos with your parents?'

'I was not a part of their plans.'

'What were their plans?'

'To party,' Gian said. 'And a late baby nearly put paid to that.'

'But it didn't?'

'No,' he admitted. 'They carried right on.'

'With a baby?'

'Without,' Gian said. 'A lot of nannies, a lot of time in Luctano… It's better this way, though. It taught me independence, so by the time they were gone, there was nothing to miss. They were never a necessary part of my life, or I of theirs.'

She could not imagine it.

Sure, her father had pulled back, but that had been in her twenties, and her mother still called her every day.

And even though she and Stefano were not as close now as they once had been, she would die if he pulled away so completely.

Even Dante, always remote and distant, was still a vital part of her world.

To have no one.

To miss no one.

'I don't believe you,' she admitted. 'I can't believe you don't miss them.'

'Truth?' Gian said, still floating in that void where there were no sides and no barriers hemming you in. 'I have missed them from the day I was born.'

'Gian?' She lifted her head when he fell silent.

'Go to sleep,' he said, but she wanted to ask him how they were supposed to be with each other in the cold light of day.

'What?' he asked her, when her head stayed up and her eyes remained focused on him.

Self-preservation struck—or was it sanity?—and Ariana, even with little experience in the bedroom, knew that pushing the issue with Gian would be something she would live to regret.

'I'm cold,' she said, though she had never felt safer or warmer.

Ariana knew when, and how, to lie.

CHAPTER ELEVEN

GIAN WOKE TO DISORDER.

Not just the knot of limbs and the scent of sex, for that he was used to, but the exposure of thoughts and the deep intimacies of last night had brought disorder into his mind.

He did not want to love her.

Ariana awoke to a cold empty bed and the sound of the shower.

She could almost feel the weight of his regret in the air.

There was no sense of regret from her. In fact, she wanted to stretch like a cat and purr at the memory of their lovemaking.

She had thought nothing could beat the first time, but again Gian had surprised her.

In his arms, as he'd driven her to the very edge and then toppled them, it had felt as if they were one.

Not now, though.

She looked over to the bedside table and the

cufflinks he had dropped last night; his tux was hanging over the suit holder.

Order had been brought to the bedroom.

Except for the hot mess that lay in his bed, Ariana thought.

Yes, an utter hot mess, because despite assurances and promises, both to Gian and herself, she had completely fallen for him.

Well, that was a given…

No, this was bigger.

This feeling was almost more than her head could contain.

It was a cocktail of affection and craving and desire and hunger but she refused, even to herself, to call it love.

It was lust, Ariana told herself.

He had turned on her senses, introduced her to her body, and she must not allow herself to believe that the kisses and intimacies shared last night were exclusively known to her.

Except it had felt as if they were.

It had felt, last night, when she had been trapped in his gaze, being kissed, being held, as if this feeling had been new to them both.

She heard the shower being turned off, and she imagined him in there naked, the mirrors all steamed up. She willed him to come out and face the woman who should not be in his bed and she hoped he wasn't wondering how to get rid of her.

Oh, God, this was going to be a million times harder than the first time. Then, it had felt like she had been party to the rules, but this time, naked in his bed, she had to find the armour to brazen out a smile and leave without revealing her heart.

He came out of the bathroom with a distinct lack of conversation and a thick white towel wrapped around his lean hips.

'*Buongiorno,*' Ariana said, and looked at Gian with his black hair dripping and unshaven face.

Unshaven, for Gian had barely been able to bring himself to look in the mirror.

He had got too close, and what had felt like a balm last night now felt like an astringent. He couldn't bear to let anyone in.

More, he couldn't bear that he was about to hurt her.

'I'll call for breakfast,' he said in a voice that attempted normality but failed. She noted that he did not get back into bed.

Ariana gave a half-laugh at his wooden response in comparison to the easy flow of words last night. 'You sound like the butler.'

He said nothing to that and Ariana pulled herself up from the bed. 'I'll have a shower.' It served two purposes: one, she refused to force a conversation on an unwilling participant and appear needy and pleading; and, two, she felt the sudden sting of tears and desperately wanted to hide it.

'Sure.' Gian said, fighting with himself not to dissuade her. He stepped back as she brushed past and he only breathed again when she closed the bathroom door.

Why the hell was he like this?

Gian generally fought introspection, but he sat on the bed and wrestled with his demons.

The panicked part of Gian wanted the maids to come in and service the apartment so he could get back his cold black heart, instead of fighting the urge to go into the bathroom and join her in the shower before spending a lazy Sunday in bed.

The buzz of his phone had him glancing at the bedside table. Luna calling at such an early hour on a Sunday morning would generally cause him to curse, yet now he leapt on the distraction and took the call.

It was not good news, to say the least.

Ariana, he knew, would freak.

When he'd ended the call, he made a couple of his own and by then Ariana had come out.

'Don't worry about breakfast,' Ariana said, her voice a little shaken, though she was clearly doing her best to control it and keep things light. She had given way to a moment of tears in the shower but she'd pulled herself together and let the hot jets of water flow over her. She would serve herself better to wait until she got home so she could weep alone.

'I'm not really hungry. I might head down to my own suite…' She wouldn't even bother putting on her gown. Wearing the robe and with wet hair, anyone who spotted her would assume she had been for a swim in the luxurious pool in the hotel spa. 'If you could just send my things down to my suite, please…'

'Ariana, wait.'

As she headed for the door, she stiffened, fighting the surge of hope that he was calling her back to apologise for the shift in mood and the silent row that had taken place. Slowly she turned around.

'It's better that you hear this from me,' Gian said, and his voice was deadly serious.

'Hear what?'

'There was a photo taken last night at the ball…'

'There were many photos taken.'

'I mean, there has been an image sold to the press. It hasn't got out yet and my team are doing all they can to suppress it, but I fear it is just a matter of time.'

'What sort of photo?'

'One of Dante…'

'Dante?' Ariana frowned. 'What has Dante got to do with anything?' Dante's behaviour had been impeccable last night. He had delivered a speech that had encapsulated the essence of their father and he had worked the room like the professional he was. Though Dante was rather well known for his rakish ways, that had all been put on hold last night.

Or so she'd thought.

'There is an image of Dante and Mia in the atrium.'

'And?' Ariana was instantly defensive. Dante was her brother after all. 'He's allowed to speak to her, for heaven's sake. He told us himself to be polite. She's my father's widow…' Her voice faded as Dante handed her his tablet and there, on an eleven-inch screen, was an image that washed away any further excuses.

Her father's very young widow was locked, groin to groin, with her elder brother, and raw, untamed desire blazed in both their eyes. Oh, she recognised that desire for what it was, because it was exactly what she had shared with Gian last night.

But Dante and Mia?

Her brother and her stepmother?

'No!' Her lungs and head shouted the denial, but the single word caught in her vocal cords and it came out a strained, husky bark. 'He would never,' she implored. 'It's been doctored, cropped…'

'Ariana, the image is real. I called Dante just now and apologised that such an invasion of his privacy took place in my hotel. My legal team are onto it, as are my security team. We are doing all we can to stop the photo getting out and,' he added darkly, 'I shall discover the culprit.'

But Ariana didn't care who had taken the photo, only that this moment in time had ever existed.

Oh, Papà!

She wanted to weep at the insult to his memory. She wanted to hurl a thousand questions at her brother, who went through women like socks. Except surely this woman, the widow of his father, should have been out of bounds?

'How long have they been together…?' Her accusing eyes looked at Gian.

'Ariana, you are asking the wrong person.'

'I'm asking exactly the right person. You're a who's who of all the scandal in Rome!' She wanted to claw the hair from her scalp. 'Did. You. Know?'

'Yes.'

He might as well have stabbed her for she put her hands to her chest and moaned exactly as if he had. 'Traitor!'

'Stop it.' Dante pointed a warning finger and moved swiftly into damage control. But this time he was moving swiftly to protect not his hotel's reputation but Ariana from the fallout that was surely to come. 'Look at me,' he said, and waited till finally she met his eyes. 'It is not so terrible.'

'But it is.'

'Because you make it so! Remember how you accused me last night, how you said Mia and I were closer in age…?'

She blinked as she replayed her own accusation.

'Your brother is my age.'

'She's his stepmother…'

'So will say the headlines, but that's just click bait… Listen to me, Ariana.' He could feel her calming just a touch. 'Think of how Dante will be feeling right now.'

She nodded, and looked down the barrel of recent weeks. 'I knew something was wrong. I thought he was just missing Papà, not just…'

'I know what you mean. Ariana, it must have been hell for him.'

'I need to speak to him.' Though still frantic, he could feel her calm beneath his touch. 'Both of them…'

'Yes,' he agreed, 'but without accusation. He and Mia have taken off to Luctano…'

'You've spoken to him.'

'Just now,' Gian said.

'Can you take me there?'

'Of course. I'll have Luna arrange the pilot.

Go down to your suite and get dressed and I'll meet you there.'

She took the elevator down to the spa floor and then stepped out and took the guest elevator back up to her own. There she pulled on some underwear and a pretty dress. Gian's calm manner was somehow infectious, for she even dried and styled her hair.

But then her phone rang and she saw it was her mother, just back from her cruise.

'How much more can I be shamed?' her *mamma* shouted.

'Mamma, please,' Ariana attempted. 'Maybe there is some explanation.'

'Mia and Dante. My son!'

'Mamma, you should surely hear what Dante has to say. They are closer in age…' Ariana pleaded, repeating Gian's words, but nothing would placate her.

'That woman!' she sobbed. 'She has killed my family, my joy, my life. She takes and she takes and she leaves me with nothing.'

'You have me,' Ariana pleaded. 'Mamma…' But she had run out of excuses for Mia and Dante. 'I'm going now to speak with him.'

'Well, you know what to say from me.'

If Ariana didn't know, she was specifically told.

'Okay?' Gian checked as they headed up to

the rooftop, except she barely heard him. All she could hear was her *mamma*'s acidic, angry words.

'I wanted the ball to be perfect for Papà.'

It was all Ariana said.

Sitting in his helicopter, Gian looked from her pale face down to the rolling hills and the familiar lace of vines. Now they were deep into spring and the poppy fields were a blaze of red, and there was foliage on the once bare vines.

He turned back to Ariana, who sat staring ahead with her headphones on, her leg bobbing up and down. He didn't doubt that she was nervous to be facing her brother.

Gian was sure that it would soon be sorted out. He knew how close the Romano siblings were. At least, they had been growing up. And surely even Ariana could understand that grief and comfort were a heady cocktail. Hell, she'd sought comfort herself on the night of the funeral after all.

He spotted the lake and soon they were coming in to land. Only then did Gian wonder how it might look that he was arriving with Ariana.

Would it be obvious they had spent the night together?

Did it announce them as a couple?

Gian was nowhere near ready for that. If anything, a couple of hours ago he'd been ready to end things, as was his usual way.

But, as it turned out, Ariana wasn't expecting anything from Gian, other than the equivalent of a rather luxurious taxi ride.

'Wait there,' she said, as she took her headphones off. 'I shan't be long.'

'What?' Gian checked, unsure what she meant.

She was more than used to entering and exiting a helicopter, and the second it was safe to do so, the door opened and the steps lowered and Ariana ran down.

'Wait…' he called, and then looked in the direction she ran.

Dante, even from this distance, looked seedy and was striding towards her, no doubt surprised by her unannounced arrival.

If Gian had thought for a moment that Ariana Romano had finally grown up, he was about to be proven wrong, for she was back to the spoiled, selfish brat of old. Only, instead of being placed over her father's knee, it was Ariana delivering the slaps.

He watched her land a vicious hit on her brother's cheek and then raise her other hand to do the same, but Dante caught it.

The scene carried echoes of another world, one Gian had loathed—champagne bottles on the floor, fights, chaos, all he had sought to erase, and the scars on his psyche felt inflamed.

Ariana heightened his senses. Gian was more than aware he had let down his steely guard in bed last night and it had shaken him. For a moment he had glimpsed how it felt to need another person, to rely on someone else, and that could never be.

Right now, though, her actions plunged him straight back into a world that had spun out of control—the chaos and fights between his parents, finding his older brother unconscious on the floor and shouting frantically for help, and their smiles and the making up that came after, the promises made that were never, ever kept.

Always they had taken things too far, and it was everything that he now lived to avoid.

'Hey.' He was speaking to the pilot, about to tell him to take off, for he wanted no part in this. Yet some odd sense of duty told him not to leave Ariana stranded, and so he sat, grim-faced, as a tearful Ariana ran her leggy way back to the helicopter and climbed in.

'We can go now,' Ariana said once her headphones and microphone were on. 'I'm done.'

And so too was he.

And he told her so the minute they stood alone back on the roof of La Fiordelise.

'You never cease to disappoint me, Ariana.'

He watched her tear-streaked, defiant face lift and her angry eyes met his as he gave her a well-deserved telling-off. 'I thought you were going there to speak with your brother, to find out how he was...'

'He shamed my mother!' Ariana shouted. 'She went on a cruise to get away from the ball and had to return to this!'

'Ah, so it was your mother talking.' He shook his head as he looked down at her, realising now what had happened between her leaving his suite and boarding the helicopter. 'And there was me thinking you had a mind of your own. How dare you put me in the middle of this? I would never have offered to take you if I'd known your plan was to behave this way.'

She had the gall to shrug. 'You have no idea what she did to us.'

'I have every idea!' Gian retorted.

'Meaning?'

But Gian was not about to explain himself. 'You know what, Ariana? I don't need your drama.'

It felt like a kind of relief that he could finally walk away without the painful struggle with his demons he had faced earlier when considering how to draw a line under all that had happened between them.

Except Ariana Romano ran after him.

He didn't want to hear her sobbing or begging for forgiveness, except Gian received neither. Instead he was tapped smartly on the shoulder and was somewhat surprised by the calm stare that met him when he turned around.

'You should be thanking me, Gian.'

'Thanking you?'

'Absolutely,' she responded. 'You were about to give me my marching orders this morning, and you were fumbling for an excuse. I handed you this on a plate.'

'You don't know that.'

'But I do.' Ariana was certain, for she could clearly recall the heavy atmosphere and the absolute certainty that Gian had been about to end things. Well, she'd given him the perfect reason to now. 'It isn't a relationship you're avoiding, Gian; it's emotion.'

Ariana struck like a cobra, right to the heart of his soul. He looked at her and all he could see was the chaos she left in her wake. He thought of the knife edge he had grown up on, the eternal threat of disaster that had hung over his family, and the eternal calm he now sought.

'Don't worry, Gian,' she said to his silence. 'I'm out of here. You keep your cold black heart and I'll carry right on.'

CHAPTER TWELVE

IT WOULD BE NICE, Ariana thought early the next morning, to pull the covers over her head as she nursed her first ever broken heart.

Officially broken.

She knew that since they had first made love she had been holding onto a dream. The fantasy that Gian would bend his rules for her and decide it was time to give love a chance…

Because it felt like love to Ariana.

Now she had to let go of that dream. Her mother called and then called again, but Ariana ignored it.

But then Stefano called and Ariana could never ignore a call from her twin…

'There's an extraordinary board meeting at nine,' he told her.

'Pass on my apologies,' Ariana mumbled, but Stefano was having none of it. 'We are to meet at the offices at eight,' Stefano told her. 'A driver has been ordered for you; he should be with you soon.'

'Eight?' Ariana checked.

'Mamma wants to speak to the three of us before the board meeting.'

'She's coming to the offices?' Ariana frowned. 'But she hasn't been there since...'

Since the news of her father and Mia's affair had broken.

This was big, Ariana knew as she quickly showered, squeezing in eye drops to erase all evidence of tears. She selected a navy linen suit and ran the straightening iron through her hair, trying to look somewhat put-together while she pondered what was about to take place. Ariana arrived at Romano Holdings and took the elevator up to where her family were waiting for her.

Her *mamma* was as pale as she had ever seen her, and Stefano looked grey. She could barely bring herself to look at Dante, but when she did she saw the bruise beneath his eye and felt sick that it had come from her own hand.

'I'm sorry,' she said to Dante. 'I just...'

'I get it,' Dante said, and gave her a hug. 'Ariana, I know how confusing this has all been, but there's something you need to hear, both you and Stefano...' He turned to their mother. 'It's time, Mamma,' he said.

* * *

This *was* big.

Gian knew that, because even as he tried to focus on his weekly planning meeting with Luna, little pings from his computer had him looking over. The press were gathered outside Romano Holdings, where an extraordinary meeting was being held, and in an unprecedented move Angela Romano was seen entering the building.

Gian watched as Ariana duly arrived in a silver car and he scanned the short piece of footage for a clue, a glimpse, as to what lay behind the mask she most certainly wore.

Her parting shot to him yesterday had seriously rattled him and he had spent most of the night simultaneously disregarding and dwelling on her words.

You keep your cold black heart and I'll carry right on.

Yet he was struggling to carry on, knowing that Ariana must be suffering now. For the first time, Gian wanted *more* information on the details of a woman's private life. He was fighting with himself not to call Ariana to see what was going on, how she was coping, what she knew...

Her brief appearance told him nothing. She was immaculate. Ariana really should be on the stage, for there was no hint of tension in her body language.

She wore a navy linen suit and her hair was smooth and tied back in a slick ponytail. She even paused and smiled her gorgeous red-lipped smile for the cameras.

'This can wait,' he told Luna, and wrapped up their morning meeting so he could focus on the news. 'If you could just bring coffee.'

'Of course.'

Throughout the morning, the little pings became more and more frequent for there was drama aplenty. Dante Romano and Mia were engaged to be married! Gian could not imagine that going down well with a certain hot-headed lady, but there Ariana was, still smiling for the cameras as she left the building and climbed into a car.

Ariana would come to him.

Of that Gian was certain.

Despite their exchange yesterday, Gian was quietly confident that Ariana would arrive in his office, because whenever there was drama in Ariana Romano's life, inevitably Luna announced she was at his door and a mini-tornado would burst in.

'Any messages from Ariana Romano?' he checked with Luna.

'None.'

'If she arrives here,' Gian said, 'please send her straight through.'

* * *

Ariana did not arrive, though, for she *refused* to run to him.

The car was mercifully cool and, rather than stare ahead, Ariana looked out of the window and smiled at the cameras as if the drama surrounding Dante and Mia hadn't affected her in the slightest. In fact, their engagement was the merest tip of an iceberg that had just been exposed to her in all its blinding glory. Ariana was having trouble taking it all in.

'Home?' the driver checked.

'No…' She hesitated, not quite ready for the emptiness of her apartment and the noise of her own thoughts. 'Just drive, please.'

She took a gulp of water from a chilled bottle the driver handed to her and tried to come to terms with the fact that her life, her childhood— in fact, all she had ever known—had been built on a lie. Her parents' marriage, of which she'd been so proud, had been a sham. They'd both had other partners and the marriage had been in name only, so much so that she and Stefano had been IVF babies.

It felt as if she was the very last to know.

They drove for ages. It was rush hour in Rome, all the workers spilling out, some rushing for transport, others taking their time for a coffee, or to sit in a bar.

She felt like an alien.

A stranger in her own body.

As they passed La Fiordelise she had never been more tempted to ask the driver to pull in, to push through the brass doors and escape to the cool calmness of Gian's office and unburden herself, as she would usually do. Except, thanks to their argument yesterday, that refuge was denied her now.

Instead, Ariana asked to be dropped off where they had walked that lonely night. She wandered there, too shocked and stunned for tears. It was a sticky late spring day and she drifted a while, ignoring the buzz of her phone.

Finally she glanced at the endless missed calls.

He came first and last.

Gian.

Mamma.

Gian.

Gian.

Mamma.

Gian.

Stefano.

Gian.

She had nothing to say to any of them, at least not until she had gathered her thoughts. Eventually, drained from walking and with a headache creating a pulse of its own, she wandered listlessly home.

'Hey,' she said to the doorman, who was dozing behind his cap. She took the elevator up, jolting when she saw a very familiar face. Gian was leaning against the wall, but came to his full height as she approached.

Her heart did not lurch in hope or relief. In fact, it sank, for right now Gian felt like another problem to deal with, another person to hide her true self from.

For her true self was hurting and dreadfully so—and her emotions were clearly too much for him.

'What are you doing here, Gian?'

'You didn't respond to my calls...'

'No.' She didn't even look at him. 'Because I was not in the mood to speak to anyone. How did you get up here?' She let out a mirthless laugh as she answered her own question. 'I really am going to fire that doorman.'

'I told him we were friends.'

'Friends.' She let out a mirthless laugh at his description of them. 'Well, however you described yourself, the doorman shouldn't have let you up.' She opened her door and her words dripped sarcasm as she invited him in. 'Come through, *friend.*'

She did not rush around making him welcome or offering a drink. Instead, she dropped her bag and headed straight to the kitchen, where she went to a drawer and took out two headache tablets and poured a glass of water.

For herself.

Gian watched as she downed the tablets and wondered how she still managed to look so put-together, even though he was sure her world had just been turned upside down. 'I saw you leaving Romano Holdings...' He tried to open the conversation, but Ariana didn't respond.

She was in no mood for conversation, and for once she didn't fill the silent gaps, offer drinks, or make him welcome. In fact, it was Gian who finally broke the tense silence.

'What happened?'

'We've been having a family catch-up and filling each other in on a few things.' She had been holding it in all day, sitting through revelation after revelation, and then a formal board meeting, always having to find a way to smile. 'Dante and Mia are expecting. That's for family's ears only,' Ariana needlessly warned, for she knew, because of his damned discretion, she might as well be telling it to the wall. 'There is to be a marriage in May, so that makes two Romano weddings.' Her voice rose and she almost let out an incredulous laugh, that both her brothers, who had always been indifferent to marriage, would soon both have all she had ever craved for herself.

But there was far more on her mind than her

brothers. 'Gian, there's a reason I didn't take your calls. I have nothing to say to you. Nothing polite anyway.' Her confusion at the unfolding events was starting to morph into anger and she turned accusing eyes on him. 'Did you know?' she asked, her eyes narrowing into two dangerous slits.

'I told you—'

'I'm not talking about Dante and Mia.' She put down the glass with such a bang that he thought it might shatter, but Gian didn't even blink. 'Did you know that my father was gay?'

'Yes.'

'For how long?'

'Since I took over the hotel, I guess.'

'You guess?' she sneered.

'I wasn't taking notes, Ariana.'

'And what about my mother's affair?'

'I knew about that too. Look, your parents didn't sit me down and tell me, but given the nature of my work, they rightfully expected discretion. I would never gossip or break a confidence. I didn't even tell Dante and he is my best friend…'

'We were lovers!' Finally she shouted. Finally a sliver of her anger slipped out. 'I had every right to know.'

'Oh, so in your perfect world the fact we were sleeping together meant we should have started holding hands and gazing into each other's eyes and *sharing*?' He spat the last word with disdain. 'Tell me, Ariana, when was I supposed to tell you? The first time we made love? The second…?'

'If we were ever to have a relationship—' She stopped herself then, her nose tightening as she fought to suppress the tears building in her eyes, because a relationship, a real one, a close one, was the very thing he didn't want. 'You could have at least told me as a friend.'

'I wanted to,' he admitted. 'But it was not my place. They were not my secrets to tell. I tried to get you to speak to your father, that day of the interview—'

'You didn't try hard enough then.' Her anger, however misplaced, she aimed directly at him. 'For two years I felt pushed away by Papà. Now I find out that he just wanted to live out his days in peace with Roberto. My God! I was led to blame Mia. I was goaded and encouraged to hate her by my mother, just because she didn't want the truth getting out.'

'Ariana…' He tried to calm her down. 'Your mother came from a time—'

'I don't care!' She swore viciously in Italian and told him what rubbish he spoke. 'I'm his daughter. I deserved to know…' He crossed over as she swallowed down a scream that felt as if it had been building since her father died. 'If I'd known the truth, I could have spent quality time with him. Had *you* told me…'

She was almost hysterical and for once he was not trying to keep a lid on the drama or stop a commotion. It was not for that reason that he pulled her into his arms, but to comfort her. But she thumped at his chest and then scrunched his perfect shirt in her fist, knowing it wasn't his fault, knowing that the truth could only have come from her father.

'It was all just a farce…' She was starting to cry now in a way she never had before. Angry, bitter tears, and Gian held her as she drowned in his arms. 'I was so proud of their marriage, but it was just a sham. Even Stefano and I were conceived by IVF to keep up the charade…' All she had just learned poured out in an unchecked torrent he allowed to flow. 'They didn't really want us…' It was then Gian intervened.

'No.'

'Yes!' she insisted. 'It was all just a sham.'

'You were wanted,' he insisted, but Ariana would not be mollified.

'You don't know that…'

'But I do.' He was holding her arms and almost shaking her in an effort to loosen her dark thoughts before they took hold. 'I know for a fact you were wanted and loved.'

'Oh, what would you know?' Ariana responded. 'What would a man like you know about love?'

'Nothing!'

She stilled in his arms at the harsh anguish in his voice.

'I know nothing about love!' He hated to tell her, for Gian was loath to share, but he would expose his soul if it saved her from the dark hole she was sinking into. 'I wasn't wanted, Ariana. I was a regretful mistake and they never let me forget that fact. When Eduardo caved to their lifestyle, I brought myself up. I could see my mother's loathing on the rare occasions she actually looked me in the eye. You know how your mother called me a beggar? Well, I was one. I walked the streets at night, just for conversation, for contact...'

Her stomach clenched in fear at the thought of a child out there alone.

'They didn't even notice or care that I was gone. You want the truth, Ariana? I wanted to disappear...'

She couldn't breathe. So passionate was his revelation that there was not even the space to take in the air her lungs craved.

'No!' she refuted. It wasn't that she thought he lied, more that she could not bear his truth.

'Yes,' he said, 'so while I have never known

love, I know what it looks like, and I know how much you were wanted and loved…'

They were the words she was desperate to hear, but she wanted to hear them from him. She was so desperate that she managed to twist her mind to pretend that Gian was saying *he* wanted her, that *he* loved her.

'Gian…' His name was a sob, a plea that she could hold onto the dream that those words were for her. Ariana honestly did not know who initiated their kiss but it was as if he read her cry in his name. For a man who knew nothing of love, he knew a lot about numbing pain. The room went dark then as their mouths melded, hot angry kisses to douse the pain. As his mouth bruised hers, as their teeth clashed, Ariana reacted with an urgency she had never known.

She kissed him as if it were vital.

And Gian kissed her to a place where only they remained. His hands were deft, shedding her jacket and lifting her top, pushing his hands up and caressing her breasts through her flimsy bra, his palms making her skin burn, then leaving her smouldering as he tackled her skirt.

He scalded her with desire, his hands hitching up her skirt so impatiently that she heard the lining rip. And Ariana, who had thought desire moved more slowly, could not begin to comprehend that she might simply seize what she craved.

He offered oblivion in the salty taste of his skin as she undid his shirt and buried her face in him. He offered escape as she unbuckled his belt and trousers.

'Ariana,' he warned, for he had not come for this. He had come to offer more, yet it was a poor attempt at a protest for he was lifting her onto the bench and tearing at her knickers as their mouths found each other again.

She had not known that the world could feel empty and soulless one moment and then find herself wrapped in his arms and drowning in the succour he gave.

He spread her thighs and she let out a shout as he pushed inside her. It was not a cry of pain but of relief, for here she could simply escape and be.

'Please,' she sobbed, because she never wanted it to end, yet they were both building rapidly to a frantic peak.

The glass she had slammed down spilled and her bottom was cold and wet, but it barely registered. There was only him, crashing against her senses again and again, a mass exodus of hurt as he touched her deep inside and somehow soothed the pain.

'Gian!' It was Ariana who offered a warning now, for she was trembling on the inside, her thighs so tight it felt like cramp. A sudden rush of electricity shot down her spine and she clenched around him, dizzied by her own pulses, and she was rewarded with his breathless shout.

They were both silent and stunned as their breathing gradually calmed. Ariana was grateful for the empty space between her thoughts. It was the first time she had felt even a semblance of quiet since her phone had shot her awake that morning. Gian too was silent, somewhat reeling at his own lack of control, for he had come here to speak, to talk, to offer Ariana comfort...

Now, though, he lowered her down from the bench and tidied himself. Ariana twisted the waistband on her skirt so the damp patch was at the side, and she even smoothed her hand over her hair, as if order could somehow be resorted.

Except it was chaos, Ariana knew, for she had made love to him again.

She had convinced herself, once again, that Gian might one day change and want her the way she wanted him.

'Ariana.' He cleared his throat. 'I didn't come here—'

'What did you come here for then?' she interrupted. 'A chat?'

'Yes,' Gian said, as the blood crept back to his head. 'A proposal.'

She looked at him with wide, nervous eyes, for this was new territory to Ariana. How one moment they could be locked in an intimate embrace, and the next attempting to speak as if his seed wasn't trickling down between her thighs. 'A proposal?'

He nodded. 'I thought a lot about what you said yesterday, and you're right, Ariana, I do avoid emotion…' He smiled a pale smile. 'Which is impossible around you.'

She swallowed, unsure where this was leading, but hoping…

Hoping!

'What you said about moving…' Gian ventured.

'I meant,' Ariana said, 'I'm not going to live in an apartment my mother feels entitled to use as a second lounge.' Her decision was crystal clear now. 'I want to take the Romano name off for a while. I want to work on myself.' She gave a hollow laugh. 'I want to actually *work*…'

'I get that,' Gian agreed. 'And, as I said, I have a proposal for you. Fiordelise Florence hotel opens at the end of May. What if you do your training here, and then work as Guest Services Manager there?'

'Sorry?' Ariana frowned, though clearly not for the reason he was thinking.

'I know I said you would start as an assistant, but I agree, you have an exceptional skill set and would be an asset.'

'Your *proposal* is a job.'

'More than a job,' Gian said.

'A career then?'

'No!' She was missing the point, Gian thought. Though he could understand why, given his usually direct style of communication. He was not good at this relationship game. 'We could see each other...*more* of each other,' he said. 'Away from your family.'

'Without them knowing?' Ariana frowned.

'Of course,' he agreed. 'We both know that would cause more problems than it would solve so we would have to be discreet. I'll have an executive manager there, so I would not be so hands-on in running the place. There would be no impropriety at the hotel and far less chance of being seen out. I would, of course, get to Florence as often as I was able.'

Oh, she understood then. 'I'd be your mistress, you mean?'

'I never said that.'

'Perhaps not in so many words, but...' Her lips were white but still turned up into the kind of practised smile she flashed for the cameras all the time, all the brighter to disguise how she was breaking down on the inside. 'Tucked away, my family in the dark, no one finding out...that sounds an awful lot like a mistress to me. Well, I won't be your Fiordelise.'

'You're complicating matters.'

'Then I'll make it simple. Where would this lead, Gian?'

'Lead?' Gian frowned. 'Why does it have to lead anywhere?'

'Because that's what my heart does.' Ariana could say it no more honestly than that. 'My heart wants to know where this might go one day.'

'I'm offering you the best parts of me, Ariana.'

'No, you're offering to keep me tucked away, to flit in and out of my life whenever it's convenient. Gian, I want my lover by my side. I want to share my life with him, not live a secret. God knows, my parents did enough of that and look how it turned out.'

'That is so you,' Gian said. 'You have to get your own way. Everything has to be now—'

'I'm not asking for now, Gian,' Ariana interrupted. 'I'm asking if there's a possibility that this might lead to more. You want directness,' she said. 'You tell your lovers up front that it will go no further. Well, I'm being direct too and I'm telling you that I want at the very least the possibility of more.'

'I have no more to give.'

She had known that getting involved with

Gian would ultimately hurt her, so why did she feel so unprepared to deal with the pain he so impassively inflicted?

'No, thank you.' Her voice was strangely high. 'Think about it...'

'I already have.' She was staring down at the barrel of a future spent mainly alone. Christmases, weddings, the birth of Dante and Mia's baby, christenings and even funerals...all the things she would have to deal with alone.

Her love unacknowledged and unnamed.

'I won't be your mistress, Gian.' Her response was clearer now, her decision absolutely made. She started to show him the door, but then changed her mind. 'Actually, before you leave, I have something I need to put to you.'

Gian frowned. He was not used to being told no in this way, particularly when he had offered Ariana more than he'd ever offered anyone. 'What?'

'I can't pretend,' Ariana said. 'And I don't want to keep making the same mistake again.'

'You think that was a mistake?' He pointed to the bench where they had both found a slice of heaven just moments ago.

'Not at that time I didn't,' Ariana said. 'Even now, no, I don't think it was, but if we make love again then, yes, that would be a mistake.'

'You make no sense.'

'I want you to stay away,' Ariana said. 'Not for ever, but at least until…' She swallowed down the words, loath to admit how he turned her on merely by his presence, how with one look, one crook of his manicured finger, she would run to him. 'Until I can act as if nothing ever happened between us.'

As if I don't love your soulless heart.

'I can't face you in front of my family until I can look at you as if nothing ever happened between us. I have to get to that place where we can do the kiss-kiss thing and…'

She took a breath to steady herself. Right now it seemed like an impossible dream, that one day she might merely shrug when she heard that Gian had arrived.

'I'd like you to stay away from my brothers' weddings…'

'I'm already not going to Stefano's, but Dante…' He shook his head. 'Dante is my closest friend…'

'Oh, please.' Ariana found a new strength in her voice then, a derisive one, a scorn-filled one. 'What would do you care about that? You've told me relationships are the very thing you don't want.'

He couldn't deny that.

'So, please, Gian.' She said it without derision now. 'If you care about me at all, then do the decent thing and stay away.'

* * *

Gian did as she asked.

He stayed away from Dante's wedding, citing an urgent issue at La Fiordelise Azerbaijan, which he had to deal with personally.

That meant Ariana could smile her red smile at the wedding and have fun with her regular posse of friends.

Yet, despite him acquiescing to her request, she missed him so much: the little flurry in her stomach that existed whenever there was the prospect of seeing him; the small shared smiles; the occasional dance; and, most of all, the prospect of a late night alone with him…

Instead, she stood in the grounds of what had once been the family home and tried to push Gian out of her heart and focus on the nuptials. Mia looked utterly gorgeous and Dante looked so proud and happy as his bride walked towards him.

'That didn't take long, did it?' Nicki nudged.

'What?'

'She's showing!' Paulo said.

Ariana pressed her lips together. Only family had been let in on the secret that Mia was pregnant. Dante had assured them all that nothing had taken place before Papà died, although for four months Mia did appear rather, well, large.

'It must have been going on for quite some

time,' Nicki whispered. 'Your pa only died in January…'

'Thanks for pointing that out,' Ariana sniped, but Nicki didn't notice for she had moved on. 'Where's Gian? I thought he'd be here.'

'I've no idea,' Ariana said, practising her shrug, as if Gian De Luca was the very last person on her mind.

As the vows were made, and Nicki jostled to take photos on her phone, Ariana asked herself why she hadn't told Nicki about what had happened with Gian. Neither had she told her the truth about her parents…

Paulo she wasn't so close to, but she and Nicki were supposed to be best friends.

It was a question of trust, Ariana realised.

Deep in her soul, Ariana realised that she did not trust the woman who sat by her side and it had nothing to do with Gian's opinion of Nicki…

The answer had arrived in its own time and the conclusion Ariana came to was all hers.

Ariana said nothing, of course. She just smiled through the proceedings and raised a glass when Dante announced in his speech that he and Mia were expecting twins—likely the reason for her showing so much. Not that Nicki corrected her earlier assumption. 'You're going to be an aunty…twice!' Nicki screeched, and called to the waiter for another bottle of champagne.

'Make that two bottles,' Paulo said, and Ariana's eyes actually scanned the room for Gian, as if hope and need might make him somehow appear.

He did not.

Apart from his absence, it was a wonderful wedding, their love so palpable it made Ariana both happy and pensive.

'It will be your turn soon.' Nicki smiled as they took a break from the dancing. 'And I shall be your bridesmaid…'

'You'll be the oldest bridesmaid in Rome if you wait for me,' Ariana said. 'I want a career.'

'Why?' Nicki frowned. 'It's not as if you need to work. You have Daddy's trust fund. Didn't he leave you an apartment in Paris? We should go there and check it out…'

'It's not enough—'

'Please,' Nicki scoffed. 'Poor little rich girl.' Her narrowed eyes snapped back to wide and friendly and she pushed out a smile. 'Let's join Paulo.'

'You go,' Ariana encouraged. 'I'll just sit here awhile.'

Her rare absence on the dance floor did not go

unnoticed. 'Get off your phone, Ariana,' Dante called. 'Come and dance...'

Except it wasn't her own phone that Ariana was going through, it was her friend's. Some might call it dishonest, or an invasion of privacy, a breach of trust...

Except, from where Ariana now sat, those titles belonged to Nicki.

There was a sneaky little shot of Mia in profile as she made her vows, a definite confirmation of the pregnancy that had been announced only to family and friends. That could be excused, though, as lots of people had been taking photos.

What could not be excused was an earlier image of Mia and Dante, locked in a passionate embrace. It was the photo that had been taken at the ball, the one that had caused so much pain.

To a heart that Ariana had thought could not be broken further, the knowledge that her friend had betrayed her added another river of pain.

The ridiculous part was that the one person in whom she would have confided, Ariana had asked not to attend.

She missed him.

Even with his selfish guidelines as to what a relationship with him might entail, she *needed* him tonight.

'Ariana!'

Her name was being shouted by lots of people now.

Maybe she had grown up some, because instead of confronting Nicki and causing a scene at her brother's wedding, she did the right thing.

Ariana put down the phone, topped up her lipstick...

...and danced.

CHAPTER THIRTEEN

ARIANA WASN'T AVOIDING sorting out her life.

If that had been the case, then she would have said yes to Gian's offer to be his mistress. She would have left her chaotic family and Janus friend and headed for Florence to be wined and dined and made love to over and over.

Instead, she faced the mountain that at first had looked far too high to climb. Yet, bit by bit, she found the tools to tackle it, some of which had been given to her by Gian.

The doorman received a stern warning that from now on Ariana's whereabouts were to remain private and heaven help him if an unannounced guest arrived at her door. She declined nights out with Paulo, *to be seen*, for she had felt Gian's exasperation and knew he was right.

It wasn't just Gian's suggestions she followed, though. She also took Dante's perpetual advice and finally turned off her phone.

Apart from Eloa's hen night, where red lips

were certainly required, most were spent sitting on her apartment floor, eating ice cream and finally sorting out her photos into albums.

Ariana chose to withdraw from the endless vacuous socialising and learned to rely on her own company, arranging her past into a more honest shape as she prepared for a new future. Finally, she was ready for a couple of nights in Luctano, where she spoke at length with Roberto and got to know her father, a little too late, but a whole lot more.

'He loved you,' Roberto said.

'I know.'

She did.

On the Thursday before she headed for home, ready now to visit his grave, Ariana spread an armful of gorgeous hand-picked daffodils, which meant truth, rebirth and new beginnings, and a little sprig of violets, for peace in the afterlife, and told him about Stefano and Eloa's wedding, which was just two days away.

'I am his wedding *padrihnos*, or wedding bridesmaid,' Ariana told her father. 'It basically means I am Stefano's best man.' She knew that would make him smile, wherever he was now. 'And Nicki is coming over tomorrow and I shall be telling her she is not welcome at the wedding and I don't want to see her any more.' Ariana swallowed. 'I still haven't told Dante about the photo.'

It wasn't her brother's wrath that worried her, more that he would, of course, tell Gian. She couldn't bear the thought of him rolling his eyes, for he had warned her about Nicki more than once.

There was something else too, something she hadn't told anyone yet, not even herself, but she admitted it out loud now. 'I am in love with Gian, Papà.'

She wouldn't be the first in her family to act in her own interests and keep it secret, were she to become his mistress, but despite how she felt about Gian, she could not reconcile herself to it. Not now she was finally becoming someone she could be proud of.

'You're not ready!' Nicki frowned, when she saw Ariana dressed in a pale grey dress and flat sandals and with her hair wild and her eyes all puffy and swollen.

'Actually, I am ready,' Ariana corrected. She had been up all night, completing the finishing touches to gifts for her loved ones, and she had worked through the day, only stopping to refuel with coffee, thinking about what must be done. 'Come in, Nicki.'

It was up there with the hardest things she had

ever done, because Ariana had truly thought of Nicki as a forever friend. Confronted with the evidence of what she had done, Nicki attacked her friend, and Ariana didn't have the energy to muster a defence against the tirade of abuse she was subjected to. Instead she listened and then said, 'I think you should leave now.'

'But we have the wedding tomorrow,' Nicki flailed. 'It'll look odd if I'm not there and we have our trip to Paris—'

'*I* have a wedding tomorrow,' Ariana interrupted. 'You're no longer welcome at Romano family events.'

It hurt and it hurt and it hurt, and once Nicki had gone, she cried for a while. But Ariana wanted this chapter of her life firmly closed, which meant that she had to tell Dante and Mia that it had been her friend who had invaded their privacy and outed them to the press.

And in turn they would tell Gian.

Only that wasn't right, Ariana knew. It wasn't up to Dante to tidy up after her. It was *her* friend who had caused this, and it was Ariana's mess to clean up. With that thought in mind, she grabbed a wrapped parcel from her bed. She had intended to mail it, but that was a cop-out and so she walked, or rather marched, her way down cobbled lanes and packed streets then pushed through the gorgeous brass door of La Fiordelise and towards his office, where she was met by his gatekeeper, Luna.

'Gian is in a meeting at the moment,' Luna said.

'It's my fault for arriving unannounced…' Ariana shook her dizzy head '…but if he can spare me a moment when he's done it would be very much appreciated.'

'Of course.' Luna nodded. 'Would you like some refreshments while you wait?'

Ariana guessed she was being sent to the Pianoforte Bar, or, as his lovers should name it, the Relegation Bar, and her braveness evaporated. 'It's fine.' Ariana had changed her mind. 'I'll catch up with him another time.'

'No, no…' Luna said, and it dawned on her that she was not being sent to the Pianoforte Bar. Instead, Luna gently suggested that she freshen up and pointed her towards a powder room. 'Still or sparkling?' she asked.

'Sorry?' Ariana frowned.

'Acqua,' Luna said patiently. 'Would you like still or sparkling?'

She must thank Luna one day, Ariana thought as she splashed her face with water and ran a comb through her hair, because she still had a morsel of pride left, enough to know she had been saved from facing him looking so terrible.

Terrible.

Ariana hadn't so much as glanced in a mirror since her confrontation with Nicki. It looked as if she'd rolled out of bed this morning and just pulled a dress on.

She had.

As if she hadn't brushed her hair.

She hadn't.

Her skin was all pale and blotchy, and her lips were swollen from crying so there was no point painting her usual red lipstick on. Still, she was grateful for the reprieve and the chance to freshen up somewhat, as Luna would no doubt have told him that yet another of his exes had shown up in a state of distress...

No, not she!

'I have Ariana Romano in Reception, asking to see you.'

Gian was just packing up his laptop, about to head to Florence. He had no time for theatrics. And yet, with each day that passed, he found that he missed the colour she had brought to his world, the drama and emotion she always brought to his table, to his bed...

He wanted them.

It had been hell missing his friend's wedding because, despite his supposed lack in the heart department, under any other circumstances he would have moved heaven and earth to have been there.

'I can tell her that you are due to fly out—'

'It's fine,' Gian cut in.

'I should warn you then, Gian, she seems distressed…'

'Was she short with you?' Gian asked, almost hopefully, because if Ariana was throwing her weight around with his staff, he could at least be aggrieved, but Luna shook her head.

'Of course not. Ariana is always polite with me.' Luna suddenly laughed.

'What's so funny?'

'Ariana always makes me smile,' Luna said. 'Anyway, I'm just letting you know that it looks as if she's been crying.'

He nodded and nudged a leather-covered box of tissues to her side of the desk in preparation for her arrival. 'Send her through.'

Gian was certain he knew what this would be about. It had been a few months since the funeral, and there had been the ball, and of course what had taken place in her kitchen. Whatever way he looked at it, Gian was sure he was about to be told he was to be a father.

Yes, there were always consequences, and not once, but on three separate occasions he had not taken the level of care he usually would, relying on her to take the Pill. It was his own fault entirely and he would handle this with grace, even if a pregnancy was everything he had always dreaded.

Gian did not know how he felt.

When she arrived in his office, she was most un-Ariana-like.

Her dress was crumpled, her espadrilles tied haphazardly, her hair, dared he say it, a day past needing a wash, and her make-up but a distant memory. And yet, to his eyes, this was the real Ariana, the one who shot straight to his heart. To see her so fragile and clearly distraught had him fighting not to go straight over and take her in his arms.

Instead, for now, he kept his arms to himself.

'Ariana.' He rose to greet her and they did the kiss-kiss routine she had referred to so painfully in their last conversation. He gestured for her to take a seat as they both tried to go back to a world where they hadn't done more. 'Can I offer you some refreshments?'

'No, no...' She shook her head. 'Thank you, though.'

'Some champagne?' Gian suggested. 'A bottle this time.'

But she did not smile at his little reference and instead shook her head. 'No, thank you.' She took a breath. It wasn't just La Fiordelise and the oasis he made that calmed her; it was Gian himself.

Despite there being so much on her mind, there was a chance to pause, to just sit in the calming low light of his office and take a moment.

That was what he gave her.

Always.

This tiny chance to pause, and it was in that moment Ariana knew that she really did want things resolved between them. No matter her blushes, it was time to face things head on.

'Before I say what I came to say—' before he got angry about Nicki '—I just want to clear the air. I'm sorry for asking you to miss Dante's wedding. It wasn't fair of me to do that.'

'There were extenuating circumstances and it was right that you did,' Gian said. 'I'm sure we'll get to managing steely politeness at family gatherings soon.'

'Yes!' She shot out a laugh and tried to glimpse a time when she wouldn't want him, but it was such an impossible thought that her smile slid away.

'Dante understood,' Gian said. 'The wedding was at such short notice. He dropped by the other day, we had lunch, and he told me about the twins. So we're all good…' He was so certain that Ariana was here to tell him she was pregnant that he kindly gave her an opening. His eyes never left her face as he watched carefully for her reaction. 'Twins must run in the family…'

'Oh, please.' Ariana gave a mirthless laugh. 'Twins don't run in my family, Gian. I assume my mother had more than one egg put back. Anything to keep up the charade!'

'It wasn't all a charade, Ariana.'

'I know that now.' She gave him a thin smile.

'Are you talking?'

'Of course we are,' Ariana said. 'I am hurt, yes, but I love her.'

Lucky Angela, Gian thought, to have her Ariana's unconditional love.

A love he himself had discarded.

'I have something for you,' Ariana told him. 'I've been sorting out some of my father's things…' She handed him a leather-bound book as she explained what she had done in recent days. 'I've made one each for my brothers and one for my mother. The contents are different in each, of course…' She was talking a little too fast, as she did when she was embarrassed, unsure if he would even want her gift.

'An album?'

'Yes, there were a lot of photos, and I thought you might like the ones you were in. But please don't look at it now: that's not what I'm here for…' She took a breath. 'Gian, there's something I have to tell you. I wasn't going to; I've tried to deal with it myself, but you do deserve to know...'

Gian braced himself to hear the inevitable.

'I've had my suspicions for a couple of weeks.' Ariana's voice was barely above a whisper, and she cleared her throat. 'I should perhaps have come to you sooner but I wanted to be sure myself...'

'You could have come to me,' Gian said. 'You can always come to me. You know that.'

'Yes.' She nodded. 'I just wanted to be very sure before I said anything, and so this afternoon I confronted her.'

Gian frowned, not sure what Ariana meant by that. 'Confronted...who?' he asked, surprised. 'What do you mean?'

'I've just come from speaking with Nicki.' Ariana ran a shaking hand through her thick dark hair and then forced herself to look at Gian and simply say it. 'It was Nicki who took the photo of Mia and Dante at the Romano Ball...'

That was it?

Ariana wasn't here to tell him she was pregnant! Instead, she had found out who had sold the photos to the press! Gian waited to catch the smile of relief that should surely be spreading over his face.

Except the smile didn't come, and the anticipated relief didn't course through his veins, as he looked at Ariana sitting tense and hurt, let down by a friend she had trusted.

'You're sure it was her?' Gian checked.

Ariana nodded. 'At Dante's wedding she was acting strangely, and when I got a chance I looked through her phone. I'm so sorry, Gian.'

'*You're* sorry?'

'Nicki was my guest on the night of the ball. I know the photo caused problems for you—'

'It's fine,' Gian cut in. 'Well, it's not, of course, but don't worry about me.' He wanted to go over and take her hands, which still twisted in her lap. 'I'm sorry she let you down.'

Ariana nodded.

'Does Dante know?'

'Not yet. It's taken me a couple of weeks to get my head around it all, and I decided I would tell you first.' She looked at the man she had always run to with troubles that seemed too big for this world. 'I might leave it until after Stefano's wedding. Really, I don't think Dante will be too upset. After all, the photo forced things out into the open. I know it angered you, though, and that it was damaging for the reputation of the hotel.'

'The only reputation that has been damaged is Nicki's,' Gian said kindly. 'What did she say when you confronted her?'

Ariana let out a pained, mirthless laugh. 'Plenty.'

He saw a fresh batch of tears flash in her eyes and knew that the confrontation hadn't been pleasant and so he asked again. 'What did Nicki say?'

'That it was my fault. That I treated her poorly and always made her feel second best...'

'No.'

But his words couldn't comfort her now. She was still shaking from the recent encounter with someone she had considered to be her friend, someone she had defended so often to this man.

'I'm sorry,' Gian said.

'I know you never liked her.'

'I mean, I'm sorry you had to go through that.'

'I should have listened to you in the first place. In fact, I'm starting to think you might be right...about the value of not letting people get too close.'

'Never take relationship advice from me,' Gian said. 'As you have undoubtedly seen, I am not particularly good at them.'

'I don't know about that.' Ariana smiled. 'You made me feel pretty wonderful, at least for a while.' But she hadn't come here to discuss her time with Gian. She'd said what she'd come to say. 'Anyway, thank you for being so gracious. I just thought it was something you should know.

I don't know if Nicki will have the audacity to come here again...'

'It'll be fine. I'll let my security team know.' He looked at her swollen eyes and knew Nicki had said plenty more. 'What else did she say?' Gian asked.

Ariana was rarely silent.

'Tell me,' he pushed.

'That I'm spoiled...'

'You deserve to be spoiled.'

'You do too, Gian.'

'What do you mean? I have everything I could possibly want or need.'

'You really don't get it, do you?' He was so self-assured and yet so remote, just so impossible to reach. She ached, literally ached, to shower him with kisses, to bring him ice cream in bed, to be there at the beginning and the end of his day... 'It's not about the best bits, Gian.' He just stared back at her, nonplussed.

It was time to let go of her fantasy that he would change his mind, that he would see her as anything more. It was time to go.

She stood to leave, but it was Gian who delayed her. 'Are you ready for the wedding tomorrow?'

'Yes.'

He wanted her to elaborate, as she usually did. Gian wanted to know if she was dreading tomorrow, if she was speaking with Mia, and lots more besides, but it would seem he had lost his front row seat to her thoughts.

'Good luck with the opening,' Ariana said.

'Thank you. Enjoy the wedding.'

'I intend to.'

This really was it, Gian realised.

The tears she had shed and her sudden appearance hadn't been about him. It had been about Nicki and a friendship lost.

There was no baby, no emotional issues to deal with, it really was just time to move on.

Gian was usually very good at that. So why did he feel this way?

The opening of La Fiordelise Florence was a tremendous success and on the Saturday night esteemed guests mingled and celebrated. While he should be quietly congratulating himself, he had never felt more alone in a crowded room.

The best food, the best champagne, and if it was sex he wanted, well, there would be no shortage there, for there were beautiful women vying for his attention.

The problem was him, because instead of enjoying the spoils of his own success Gian found himself slipping away not long after dinner, sitting in his impressive suite leafing through a leather-bound book... There were several pictures of him fishing or riding with Dante and later with the twins. There was one of a teenage Gian rolling his eyes while Dante kicked a stone to Stefano as a very spoiled Ariana sat on a fat little pony, the absolute apple of her parents' eyes.

But then Ariana faded from the images as life took its twists and turns and he had headed to university. There were a couple of years without any images while the disasters that had unfolded back then had played out.

He had never really likedAngela Romano, but there was a picture of him smiling at her the night La Fiordelise had been saved. Angela was dripping jewels and being her usual affected self, as she stood with her husband and Gian.

This really was a gift without an agenda, Gian knew, for there was even a picture of Gian standing with the Romano family on the night Ariana had attended her first ball. He knew Ariana had made this album purely for his benefit because she would prefer that this picture of herself be relegated to burn in a fire for she looked scowling and awkward.

It was a slice of time he had forgotten.

Even now, as he looked at the photo, there was no flash of memory.

He would have been in his mid-twenties then, and Ariana at that awkward age of fifteen, her hair done in a way that now looked very much of its time, and she had been wearing too much make-up.

They had all been there for him throughout his life, and he couldn't help but wonder what each of the Romanos was doing now.

How Ariana was coping with the nuptials.

He turned back the pages and looked again at a podgy little Ariana sitting on a podgy little pony, only he saw it differently this time... Not the pony, or the pampered heiress, just the absolute adoration on her face as she smiled at her parents and pleaded with them, with her eyes, to be loved, loved, loved...

It could have been a cone full of chestnuts they had given her; it wasn't the pony she had craved, it had been attention and love.

Gian went out onto the balcony and gazed on the Ponte Vecchio, the gorgeous old bridge that was the soul of Florence, and sung about in 'O Mio Babbino Caro'.

Yet it was not the music that filled his soul tonight, for he would never look at this bridge and not think of her.

Ariana.

Yes, he was proud of his new hotel, but tonight his heart was in Rome.

CHAPTER FOURTEEN

'COLOUR,' ELOA HAD SAID.

A Brazilian wedding was a colourful affair, and that was evident even before the nuptials had started. Even though Gian was not in Rome this weekend, he had ensured La Fiordelise was at their disposal. The reception area was a blaze of colour and forbidden perfume, Ariana noticed as she walked through Reception and headed up to her suite to get changed.

Ariana would have preferred to wear black, as she had to the Romano Ball, to denote that she was in mourning. For her father, of course, but the end of a relationship also felt a whole lot like grief. She awoke with a weight of sadness in her chest that never quite left, and she felt Gian's presence beside each and every thought. Yet she must push it all aside today, so she chose a dress as red as her signature lipstick. She wore her jet-black hair up, teased, with a few stray curls snaking down, meaning that she looked far more vibrant than she felt.

As Stefano fiddled with his tie, Ariana stepped out for a moment onto the balcony and looked down at the square beneath and remembered the night of her father's funeral, that desperately lonely night made so much better by Gian.

Why had she insisted that he stay away, when the truth was that she missed him already?

Half the congregation were clipping their way across the square to the venue and Ariana watched the colourful display from the balcony of Stefano's suite. The sun seemed at odds with the greyness of her world, and the flowers looked like placards from angry protesters to her tired eyes, yet they waved their petals and demanded she sparkle.

And so Ariana put on her best smile and stepped back inside. 'We should head over soon,' she told him.

'Before we do, there's something I want to say,' Stefano said. 'Ariana, I'm sorry for shutting you out.'

'Stefano, we don't need to do this now. It's your wedding day…'

'And I want it to be perfect,' he said. 'I want the air to be cleared between us. Gian suggested—'

'Gian?' Ariana frowned.

'He called me this morning to wish me well and apologise for not being here. We got to talking...' He took a breath.

Even though he wasn't physically here, Gian was still looking out for her, Ariana realised. He was still fixing the pieces of her life that he could, and she was so grateful to him as Stefano spoke on and finally gave her his reasons for keeping his distance. 'You see, I knew Mamma was having an affair, and I was having suspicions about Pa and Roberto. I was worried I might let things slip when I spoke to you and so I stayed away as much as I could. I was wrong...'

'No,' Ariana corrected. 'You did what you thought best at the time, and the air is clear now.' Clear, if a little thick with unshed tears when she thought of Gian and this moment he had created to bring her and her twin back together.

'We have some catching up to do,' Stefano prompted.

'We do...' Ariana smiled '...though it can wait till after your honeymoon.' But certain things would wait for ever. They were close again, but it would never be like it was before. Gian had changed her, she realised. She was far more independent now and did not need to run and tell Stefano everything, certainly not about herself and Gian.

It was her secret to keep.

'Do you have the rings?' Stefano asked for maybe the twentieth time.

'I have the rings.' Ariana smiled as she checked again for maybe the thirtieth time! 'Are you nervous?'

'Very,' Stefano admitted, and looked at his sister. 'I miss him.'

'I know you do.'

'It's the bride who should be crying...' Stefano said as he took a deep breath. 'I'm so happy yet I miss him so much today.'

'Hey,' Ariana soothed, and then she did something she never thought she would do. She reached into her purse and took out a tiny sliver of gold she had sworn she would never give away, but that Gian had told her she might. 'Papà gave Gian this for strength when his family died...'

'Really?'

'And he gave it to me when I felt weak at Papà's funeral, but I don't need it any more.' She put it in his top pocket. 'Papà is with you today.'

Ariana got on with her designated job: getting her brother to the embassy on time and remembering the rings.

Eloa was a stunning bride and the day brimmed with happiness. Well, that was what Ariana determinedly showed, even if there was a squad of elves holding down the cork on a vat of tears she would later shed.

'No Nicki?' Dante checked after the service as he handed her a glass of cachaça—a rather smoky Brazilian rum that made her eyes water. Ariana shook her head, deciding that she would tell him another time about the photo.

Tonight was a celebration after all.

And then Mia had a question for her new husband. 'No Gian again?'

'His new hotel,' Dante said. 'The opening was booked before the wedding date was decided and couldn't be changed...'

It was a throwaway sentence as he took his gorgeous wife off to dance and Ariana stood there, wondering how she would get through not just tonight but every future Romano family event at which Gian should be present.

Because Mia was right, Gian should be here.

The Romanos loved him like their own and he belonged here amongst them.

And when the next one happened, and the next, Ariana had to somehow work out how *not* to tumble into bed with him afterwards.

For. The. Rest. Of. Her. Life.

Oh, those elves were working overtime, yet she refused to cry and so she danced with Pedro, who was a cousin of the bride, and she danced with Francisco, who was a friend of an aunt, and Ariana laughed and danced and determinedly refused to give in to a heart that was breaking.

'Come on, Ariana…' They were all dragging her to the centre, where it would seem it was a Brazilian tradition to dance around Eloa's gold shoes. Really, Ariana had no idea what she was doing, but she swayed her hips and laughed and did a sort of Spanish flamenco around the shoe, tapping her feet and swishing the ruffles on her dress.

He had almost missed this, Gian thought when he saw her.

He had almost missed another Romano wedding and another night with people he could only now admit to himself were family.

The usually unruffled Luna had nearly thrown a fit when Gian had declared that he was flying back to Rome and asked if she could arrange it urgently, as well as a couple of other small assignments he wanted her to swiftly organise. 'I need to be there tonight.'

Fortunately, Ariana had arranged the reception just across from La Fiordelise so, with his helicopter landing late into the night, it was a simple matter of checking everything was in place and feeding some official documents through the shredder.

Gian didn't need reminders of the past.

It was a future he wanted now.

And with the past shredded, he walked across

the square to Palazzo Pamphili and found, to his pleasant surprise, he was still on the guest list.

Walking through the grand building with its intricate ceilings and formal galleries, there was a moment to gather himself in such esteemed surroundings. It felt deserted, yet finally he could hear the laughter and merriment as if calling for him to join in. And even without his feelings for Ariana, it was right that he was there tonight for, perfect or not, these people had been more of a family to him than his own.

'Gian!' Dante caught up with him as he congratulated the bride and groom and apologised for arriving so late. 'It is good that you made it.'

It was said completely without implication or malice that he had missed theirs, Gian knew; Dante and Mia were simply pleased to see him.

Gian was back in the fold, as easily as that, and he stood watching the celebrations for a moment, taking it all in. He did not have to strain to locate Ariana; she was completely unmissable, of course.

Dressed in red, she was the belle of the ball, dancing and laughing and having the time of her life, so much so that even Gian could not see the hurt he was certain resided within.

He wasn't vain enough to believe it was all to do with him. There was the loss of her father, her relationship with her mother, Nicki, Stefano…

He was proud of his diva and her acting skills, proud of her resilience, and also aware of an unfamiliar sensation tightening his chest as she danced happily in another man's arms.

And another!

Damn it, Ariana, Gian thought, *I get it. Your life will go on without me, but please tone it down!*

He had never cared about anyone enough to know jealousy before, yet he learned there and then to breathe through it, even smiling as she kicked up her heels.

No longer able to resist, he caught Ariana's arm as she stamped past him, and saw how startled she was in her violet eyes when they locked with his.

Gian was here.

Damn!

Just as she did her best to move on and prove to herself she could party without him, the best-looking spanner in the world was suddenly thrown into the works.

'I'm busy dancing,' she told him, and reclaimed her arm.

'It's a Brazilian wedding, Ariana,' he told her. 'Not a Spanish one.'

'I know that.'

'Yet you're doing the flamenco.'

'So I am…' Her heart was hammering because she could not quite believe that he was here. 'These cachaças are very strong.' She was trying to act normally, or rather how she would have acted a year ago at a family event when Gian De Luca suddenly showed up. 'I thought you had to be at the La Fiordelise Florence, opening—'

'I left early and gave myself the rest of the night off...'

'Why are they all called La Fiordelise?' she snapped. It had always annoyed her and she let him know tonight. 'It's hardly original.'

'Your father said the same.'

'Well, you should have listened to him. La Fiordelise, London. La Fiordelise, Azerbaijan...' *Gosh those cachaças must be strong*, she thought, because she allowed a little of her resentment to seep out. 'Perhaps you could send me there...'

He just smiled.

But it was a smile she had never seen before. Not his on-duty smile, or his off-duty one; it was just a smile that let her be, that simply accepted her as she was and, she felt, suddenly adored.

'Hey, Ariana...' Pedro was waving her to join in another odd-looking dance.

'Your boyfriend is calling you to dance with him again,' Gian said, and with those words let her know he'd been watching her for a while. 'You're very popular tonight.'

'Yes, I am,' Ariana said, and she'd never been happier to be caught dancing and smiling and laughing, even if she was bleeding inside. 'I am in demand!'

'Have you time to dance with me?'

No.

She had to practise saying no to him, had to have that tiny word fall readily from her tongue.

For. The. Rest. Of. Her. Life.

Except that tiny word felt far too big when she looked into those beautiful slate-grey eyes. She would start tomorrow, Ariana decided, and allow herself just one tiny dance tonight. 'One dance,' Ariana said, and found herself back in his arms. 'For the sake of duty.'

Yet this was no duty dance, for his arms were no longer wooden and his hands ran down her ribs and came to rest on her hips and there was slight pressure there to pull her against him. He moved like silk and this time it was Ariana who was the one holding back.

'Dance with me,' he moaned.

'I am.'

'Like we did.'

'No,' she said. 'My mother is looking.'

'Let her look.'

'You know what she can be like.'

'Tell her that your sex life is none of her business.'

'I have.' Ariana laughed. 'But we no longer have a sex life, so there's nothing to tell.'

She felt the heat of his palm low on her hips and heat somewhere else as he pulled her hard up against him. His voice was low in her ear and made her shiver. 'You're sure about that?'

This wasn't fair, Ariana thought as they danced cheek to cheek with their bodies meshed together. He wasn't being fair after all that had passed between them.

'They will guess...' Ariana started.

'Stop worrying about them,' Gian said, and for a little while she did. Her family all danced with their various partners and she danced with a man who was always there for her. There was something so freeing about Gian's acceptance of her, and the way he lived life on his terms. It was something she was starting to embrace herself and so she wrapped her arms around his neck and told him a little of her new world. 'I've told my lazy doorman that he's not allowed to let guests up without my permission, not even my mother, and I shall petition the other residents to have him removed if he doesn't improve.'

'Good for you.'

'And I have an interview next week with your rival company. I used my mother's maiden name, so I know I got the interview on my own merit.'

'Very good,' Gian said.

'And I will never give up on love.'

'I'm pleased to hear it.' He was serious suddenly. 'Can we go outside?'

'It will cause too much gossip and rumour...'

'I don't care.'

'Well, I do,' Ariana said. 'I'm not leaving Stefano's wedding to make out with you.'

'That is a revolting term,' Gian told her, 'but fair enough.' For though he was desperate to speak with her, she was right not to leave during her brother's wedding reception. 'Will you come over to La Fiordelise afterwards?' Gian asked.

'No...' she said slowly. Her reply was tentative, but with practice she would perfect it, Ariana decided. 'No.' She said it more clearly this time.

No. No. No.

Easy as pie.

'Come to me tonight.'

They were still cheek to cheek, though the music had ended, yet they carried on dancing. She could feel herself weakening at his touch. 'No,' she told him as he reached into his inner pocket and slipped a cold thin card where the ruffle of her dress parted. It was all discreetly done, yet Ariana knew she should have slapped him there and then, but lust moved faster than anger where Gian De Luca was concerned. It took a moment for her to form the proper reply. 'Leave me alone, Gian.'

'I can't.'

'Ariana!' Her *mamma* was laughing and calling her over. 'Gian!' In fact, she was calling them both, for the music had restarted and upped its tempo and the bride and groom were about to be waved off into the night.

It was loud, it was fun, and it was over.

Stefano and Eloa were officially married and it was kisses and final drinks and then they all spilled out of the venue into the square. She was so happy for Stefano and Eloa, especially now the air had been cleared between her and her twin.

And happy for Mia and Dante too, Ariana thought as she watched them walk hand in hand into the night.

If it was possible to be lonely and happy at the same time, then she was lonely and happy for herself too, for Gian had already gone.

She wanted not just to be part of a couple, but she wanted to be part of that couple with Gian.

Walking hand in hand in public, kissing without secrets, in love for all to see.

The square had never looked more beautiful. There was a carousel all lit up and the stunning fountains were gushing and spouting. It was a special place indeed, where they had eaten hot chestnuts on the night she'd said farewell to her father, and where she now stood so confused and so wanting to go into La Fiordelise if it meant another night with the man she loved.

She would always want him.

That was a given.

If, somehow, forty years from now, they were here at Stefano and Eloa's ruby wedding celebration, there would still be a longing and an ache for what could have been. If learning the truth about her family had taught her anything, it was that regrets were such a waste of a life. She didn't want to have any regrets when it came to Gian.

She would start saying no on Monday.

Not caring if she was found out, Ariana slipped away and found herself in the reception area of La Fiordelise, heading straight for his bed and the bliss he would temporarily give.

Life was better with Gian in it than not.

Yes, she was turning into Fiordelise, Ariana decided as she took the elevator up.

He opened the door and, before she fell into his arms, she stated her case. 'There will be rules,' Ariana said.

If she was to be his mistress then there would be rules and *she* would be the one making them.

'We shall discuss them,' Gian agreed.

'If you cheat on me, you die.'

He laughed. 'I'm saving you from prison then. I never cheat.'

'Liar.'

'Never. Even at your interview when I wanted to kiss you but Svetlana—'

'Stop!' She halted him. 'Don't ever try to redeem yourself with another woman's name.' She was way too needy to ignore it though. 'You wanted to kiss me then?'

'All over,' he told her. 'Come, there's something I want to show you…'

Down his hallway they went and she smiled when she saw there were pictures of Gian. 'When did you do this?' she asked.

'Tonight. The maintenance man has been busy.'

'Oh, Gian.' Her eyes were shining and happy to see his childhood finally featured on the wall, but then her smile died. 'What the hell is this doing here?' It was the most appalling, awkward photo of her at her first Romano Ball. She had been tempted to tear it up, but had decided it wasn't just her memory to delete.

'No!' She was appalled. 'That photo was for your eyes only, I look terrible!'

'You do and, believe me, your mother had nothing to worry about then… It was here that things started to change for me…'

Her breath stopped, as there she was, in a silver dress, standing next to Gian, in an informal shot of a night that had been more difficult than the picture revealed.

It was the first Romano Ball without her *papà*. He had been a last-minute withdrawal due to a deterioration in his health. On the one hand, she had been relieved that she wouldn't have to see him with Mia.

On the other hand, it had meant her *papà* was getting worse.

Gian had steered her through it, though. He always did.

He had held her in those wooden arms and told her that she was doing well, and it had meant the world.

'I think,' Gian said, 'well, I know, that for me things changed that night…' She swallowed as he went on. 'You were right. I easily remembered what you were wearing, for my eyes barely left you that night, and I think things changed for you too, Ariana. You didn't come by my office so much after that…'

'No…' She flushed as she admitted to herself something that for so long she had denied. 'I have liked you for a lot longer than you realise, than even I dared admit.'

'Come,' he said, 'I have something for you.'

Of course that something was in the direction of the bedroom, and as they walked there, she said, 'I'll make a terrible mistress, Gian. I talk too much, I'm not very discreet...' But then her voice trailed off for there on the bed lay everything she had once thought she wanted: a blush tartan suit, a silk cowl-necked cami, a string of pearls and even a little wallet for her business cards.

'Gian...' She wanted to weep, for he made her so weak.

This time when he unzipped the back of her dress, his fingers lingered and she closed her eyes as he peeled it off and slowly kissed her shoulder.

'Turn around,' he said in that voice that made her shiver. She was a little bewildered and a lot in lust as she complied.

He undressed and then dressed her.

She lifted her arms as he slid on the silk cami, and she lifted her feet as he negotiated the little kilt. The only resistance was in her jaw as he put on the jacket, for it was everything she had wanted, and yet Ariana knew she deserved more.

He dressed her neck in a string of pearls and she closed her eyes as he secured the clasp, then turned her around and knelt as he dressed her feet in the gorgeous neutral stilettoes that his guest managers wore. 'We can't work together, Gian.'

'We can.'

'No, because I'm not going to spend my career worrying about when my time will be up...'

'It will never be up.'

But Ariana had too much to say to stop and listen. 'I don't want to be hidden away, and I don't want hide my love.'

'You won't be hidden away,' Gian said. 'And you don't have to hide a single thing.'

'It would be unprofessional,' Ariana insisted, 'to be sleeping with a member of your staff.'

'I think it would be perfectly reasonable for the owner to love his wife, who just happens to be a guest services manager.'

She swallowed and then corrected him. 'VIP Guest Services Manager.'

'Absolutely.' He smiled. 'Ariana, Duchess of Luctano, VIP Guest Services Manager...'

'Stop.'

'Well, we might leave off the title on your business card...' He looked at her frowning face. 'I'm asking you to marry me.'

'Please, stop,' Ariana said, for she did not want him playing games with her heart.

'No,' Gian said, and from the bedside drawer he took out a box she recognised. 'I don't want to stop, and I don't want my lineage to end. I want ours to be a different legacy...'

She looked at the most beautiful ring, in shades of pomegranate, and it was so unexpected, but not as unexpected as what he said next. 'When you walked into my office yesterday, I thought it was to tell me you were pregnant...'

'Gosh, no.'

'I think I wanted you to be.'

Her world went still as that black heart cracked open and revealed all the shining hope for their future inside.

'I don't want to be like that old fool who left it too late,' Gian said. 'I want the woman I love by my side. I love you,' Gian clarified, and she felt the blood pump in every chamber of her heart as it filled with his words. 'You are the most important person in my day.'

It was the one thing Ariana had wanted her whole life—to be the centre of someone's world, to be wanted, to be cherished, for exactly who she was.

'Ariana,' Gian said, 'you are the love of my life. Will you be my wife?'

Her answer was a sequence of squeaks, a 'Yes,' followed by 'Please,' as an ancient ring slid onto a slender finger, and because it was Ariana, she took a generous moment to properly admire it. 'I love it,' she said, and he watched massive pupils crowd the violet in her eyes. He adored her absolute passion for his ring. 'You would never have sold it...' She scolded the very thought.

'No,' he said, 'it belongs with me, as do you.'

He was silenced by her kiss, a kiss that held nothing back but showered him in frantic love. Another 'I do, I do,' she said, and then followed that with another needy, necessary question. 'When?' she asked. 'When can we marry?'

'Soon,' Gian said, and got back to kissing her, but Ariana had something else on her mind.

'And can we have…?'

'You can have the Basilica, if you want it,' Gian said.

'No,' Ariana said, 'can we have tutti-frutti and salted chestnut ice cream for dessert…?'

He laughed. 'Trust you to have chosen the dessert by the end of the proposal.' And then he kissed her to oblivion, and behind closed doors he took his newly appointed guest services manager and made love to her as the Very Important Person she was.

To him.

For life.

EPILOGUE

'YOU HAVE ANOTHER phone call.' Gian gently shook a sleeping Ariana's shoulder. 'Stefano,' Gian added, watching her eyes force themselves open, knowing she could never not take a call from her twin.

And certainly not on an important day such as this.

'*Stai bene?*' Stefano urgently asked if she was okay.

'Of course.' Ariana smiled sleepily as she sat herself up in bed. 'We are doing wonderfully.'

'Have you decided on a name for her?' Stefano asked.

'We are waiting until you arrive to announce the name,' Ariana said. 'I want us all to be together when we do.'

Eloa and Stefano and little George were in Brazil and soon to board a flight to Florence. Dante, Mia and the twins would fly in with their mother and Thomas tomorrow, and all would meet the newest member of the family. But, tired from an exhausting day, Ariana was grateful that for now it was just the three of them.

'How is Stefano?' Gian asked when she ended the call.

'Excited to meet her,' Ariana said, gazing over to the little crib that held their sleeping daughter.

She was so beautiful, with dark hair and a little red face, and tiny hands with long delicate fingers.

They were both aching for her to wake up just to look into those gorgeous blue eyes again and hear her tiny cry.

'I wish Papà had got to see her,' Ariana said. Her father was the only part of her heart that was missing. 'I wish he had known about us.' She would get used to it, of course, but she couldn't help but think how happy he would be today. 'I am glad we had her in Florence,' Ariana said. 'I feel closer to him here.'

'I know you do.'

La Fiordelise Rome was no longer where Gian resided. For the first time he had a home—a real one—a luxurious villa just a little way out of Florence, with a gorgeous view of the river.

This morning, as labour had started, Ariana had stood on the terrace, taking in the morning, the pink sky, and the lights starting to go off in the city they both loved and thinking what a beautiful day this was for their baby to be born.

And now she was here and it was right to have a little cry and to miss her *papà*.

'I have something for you,' Gian said, and he went into his pocket and pulled out a long, slim box. But instead of handing it to her, he opened it and took the slender chain out and held up the pendant for her to see.

She smiled as he brought it closer, but she didn't immediately recognise what it was.

'Gian?' she questioned as she examined the swirl of rose gold and saw that instead of an F for Fiordelise, there was an A, sparkling in diamonds. 'It's beautiful, but…'

'Take a look,' Gian said, and he pulled back the heavy drapes that blocked out the world and the city skyline. Her eyes were instantly drawn to the sight of La Fiordelise Florence, for it was lit up in the softest pink.

And there was something else different.

The elegant signage had been changed. Oh, there was still the familiar rose gold swirl, but like her pendant the letter in the centre was now an A.

'The hotel has had a name change,' Gian said. 'It is now Duchessa Ariana.'

'But…' She was overwhelmed, stunned actually, that this private man would share their love with the world.

'I've been planning it for months,' Gian said. 'Even the letterhead has all changed. The last time I saw your father, like you, he told me I could do better with the hotel names and, like me, he thought your name should be in lights. I think he knew the way the wind was blowing, perhaps even before we did.'

She liked that thought so very much, and then, better than any insignia, came the sweetest sight of all: their daughter stretching her little arms out of the swaddle of linen. They both smiled at the little squeaking noise she made.

Gian clearly wasn't going to wait for her to cry.

'Hey, Violetta,' he said, and gently lifted her from the crib.

They had named her after her great-great-grandmother, the forgotten Duchess, somehow lost in all the tales of Fiordelise.

Well, she was forgotten no more.

Violetta's restored picture was mounted on the gallery wall of their home in Rome, and soon it would be joined by her namesake's first photo.

Ariana buried her face in her daughter's and breathed in that sweet baby scent, and then lifted her head and gazed down at her.

'I cannot believe how much I know her already,' Ariana said, playing with her tiny fingers, 'and at the very same time I cannot wait to get to know her more…'

That was, Gian thought as he looked at his wife, a rather perfect description of his love.

* * * * *

Couldn't get enough of
The Italian's Forbidden Virgin?
Discover the first instalment in the
Those Scandalous Romanos duet
Italy's Most Scandalous Virgin*!*

And catch these other stories
by Carol Marinelli!

The Billionaire's Christmas Cinderella
Claimed for the Sheikh's Shock Son
The Sicilian's Surprise Love-Child
Secret Prince's Christmas Seduction

Available now!